PRAISE FOR

# DIANA PALMER

"Nobody tops Diana Palmer when it comes
to delivering pure, undiluted romance.
I love her stories."
—*New York Times* bestselling author
Jayne Ann Krentz

"Diana Palmer is a mesmerizing storyteller who
captures the essence of what a romance should be."
—*Affaire de Coeur*

"Diana Palmer is a unique talent
in the romance industry. Her writing combines
wit, humor, and sensuality; and,
as the song says, nobody does it better!"
—*New York Times* bestselling author
Linda Howard

"No one beats this author for sensual anticipation."
—*Rave Reviews*

"A love story that is pure and enjoyable."
—*Romantic Times Magazine* on
*Lord of the Desert*

"The dialogue is charming,
the characters likable and the sex sizzling…"
—*Publishers Weekly* on *Once in Paris*

Dear Reader,

International bestselling author Diana Palmer needs no introduction. Widely known for her sensual and emotional storytelling, and with more than forty million copies of her books in print, she is one of the genre's most treasured authors. And this month, Special Edition is proud to bring you the exciting conclusion to her SOLDIERS OF FORTUNE series. *The Last Mercenary* is the thrilling tale of a mercenary hero risking it all for love. Between the covers is the passion and adventure you've come to expect from Diana Palmer!

Speaking of passion and adventure, don't miss *To Catch a Thief* by Sherryl Woods in which trouble—in the form of attorney Rafe O'Donnell—follows Gina Petrillo home for her high school reunion and sparks fly.… Things are hotter than the Hatfields and McCoys in Laurie Paige's *When I Dream of You*— when heat turns to passion between two families that have been feuding for three generations!

Is a heroine's love strong enough to heal a hero scarred inside and out? Find out in *Another Man's Children* by Christine Flynn. And when an interior designer pretends to be a millionaire's lover, will *Her Secret Affair* lead to a public proposal? Don't miss *An Abundance of Babies* by Marie Ferrarella—in which double the babies and double the love could be just what an estranged couple needs to bring them back together.

This is the last month to enter our Silhouette Makes You a Star contest, so be sure to look inside for details. And as always, enjoy these fantastic stories celebrating life, love and family.

Best,
Karen Taylor Richman
Senior Editor

Please address questions and book requests to:
Silhouette Reader Service
U.S.: 3010 Walden Ave., P.O. Box 1325, Buffalo, NY 14269
Canadian: P.O. Box 609, Fort Erie, Ont. L2A 5X3

# DIANA PALMER

## THE LAST MERCENARY

Silhouette®

SPECIAL EDITION™

Published by Silhouette Books

America's Publisher of Contemporary Romance

In memoriam, Brenda Lou Lilly Rogers.
My friend.

SILHOUETTE BOOKS

ISBN 0-373-24417-7

THE LAST MERCENARY

Copyright © 2001 by Diana Palmer

This edition published by arrangement with Harlequin Books S.A.

® and TM are trademarks of Harlequin Books S.A., used under license. Trademarks indicated with ® are registered in the United States Patent and Trademark Office, the Canadian Trade Marks Office and in other countries.

Visit Silhouette at www.eHarlequin.com

Printed in U.S.A.

## Books by Diana Palmer

Dear Reader,

This is the third book in the new trilogy of mercenary novels Silhouette was kind enough to let me do. I really enjoyed writing the original mercenary series back in the eighties, and I got to revisit some of the characters in these books. I hope you have enjoyed the new SOLDIERS OF FORTUNE series as much as I have enjoyed writing it for you. This is, in many ways, the most exciting of the three stories, because in it Callie Kirby helps Micah Steele lure the drug lord, Lopez, into a trap. In the process, Callie and Micah discover that the danger Lopez presents is equal to the danger of giving in to temptation. Can an independent woman settle for a man who has never known compromise—and can a mercenary give up the adrenaline rush of his lifestyle for the serenity of a small Texas town? Read the book and find out.

Micah Steele has appeared in several books, including my MIRA Books title, *Paper Rose,* and I thought he needed a longer book than the other mercenaries because of his complicated personal life—so he gets a Special Edition novel. I also like the chance to have an exotic location or two, particularly the Bahamas, where I have spent some of the loveliest days of my life. Nassau is such a beautiful blend of past and present, and I have a very special memories of watching the little tugboats turn the big passenger ships in the harbor, and walking through the straw market at Prince George Wharf.

Not that Texas has any less impact in my memories! I have seen the cattle market at Fort Worth, and I have stood where Bowie and Travis and Crockett stood and died. I have seen vast ranches and majestic cities. And I have loved even the smallest of the small Texas towns.

I have tried to show these wonderful places as I first saw them, with the same awe and sense of delight and wonder that I felt.

I hope you enjoy *The Last Mercenary,* and the surroundings where the story unfolds. As always, thank you so much for all your kindness and caring over the years. When you have a minute, stop by and visit me at www.dianapalmer.com or write me in care of Silhouette Books. I am slow to answer mail, but, oh, how I love to get it!

Love,

Diana Palmer

# Chapter One

It had been a jarring encounter.

Callie Kirby felt chilled, and it wasn't just because it was November in south Texas. She watched the stepbrother she worshiped walk away from her as casually as if he'd moved around an obstacle in his path. In many ways, that was what Callie was to Micah Steele. He hated her. Of course, he hated her mother more. The two Kirby women had alienated him from the father he adored. Jack Steele had found his only son wrapped up in the arms of his young wife—Callie's mother—and an ugly scene had followed. Callie's mother, Anna, was sent packing. So was Micah, living mostly at his father's home while he finished his last year of residency.

That had been six years ago, and the breach still hadn't healed. Jack Steele rarely spoke of his son. That suited Callie. The very sound of his name was painful to her. Speaking to him took nerve, too. He'd once called her a gold digger like her mother, among other insults. Words could hurt. His always had. But she was twenty-two now, and she could hold her own with him. That didn't mean that her knees didn't shake and her heartbeat didn't do a tango while she was holding her own.

She stood beside her little second-hand yellow VW and watched Micah bend his formidable height to open the door of the black convertible Porsche he drove. His thick, short blond hair caught the sunlight and gleamed like gold. He had eyes so dark they looked black, and he rarely smiled. She didn't understand why he'd come home to Jacobsville, Texas, in the first place. He lived somewhere in the Bahamas. Jack had said that Micah inherited a trust fund from his late mother, but he'd sounded curious about his son's luxurious lifestyle. The trust, he told Callie privately, wasn't nearly enough to keep Micah in the Armani suits he wore and the exotic sports cars he bought new every year.

Perhaps Micah had finished his residency somewhere else and was in private practice somewhere. He'd gone to medical school, but she remembered that there had been some trouble in his last year of his residency over a lawsuit, stemming from a surgical procedure he refused to do. Neither she nor his father knew the details. Even when he'd been living with his father, Micah was a clam. After he left, the silence about his life was complete.

He glanced back at Callie. Even at a distance he looked worried. Her heart jumped in spite of her best efforts to control it. He'd had that effect on her from the beginning, from the first time she'd ever seen him. She'd only been in his arms once, from too much alcohol. He'd been furious, throwing her away from him before she could drag his beautiful, hard mouth down onto hers. The aftermath of her uncharacteristic boldness had been humiliating and painful. It wasn't a pleasant memory. She wondered why he was so concerned about her. It was probably that he was concerned for his father, and she was his primary caretaker. That had to be it. She turned her attention back to her own car.

With a jerk of his hand, he opened the door of the Porsche, climbed in and shot off like a teenager with his first car. The police would get him for that, she thought, if they saw it. For a few seconds, she smiled at the image of big, tall, sexy Micah being put in a jail cell with a man twice his size who liked blondes. Micah was so immaculate, so sophisticated, that she couldn't imagine him ruffled nor intimidated. For all his size, he didn't seem to be a physical man. But he was highly intelligent. He spoke five languages fluently and was a gourmet cook.

She sighed sadly and got into her own little car and started the engine. She didn't know why Micah was worried that she and his father might be in danger from that drug lord everyone locally was talking about. She knew that Cy Parks and Eb Scott had been instrumental in closing down a big drug distribution center, and that the drug lord, Manuel Lopez, had reputedly targeted them for revenge. But that didn't explain Micah's connection. He'd told her that he tipped law enforcement officials to a big drug cargo of Lopez's that had subsequently been captured, and Lopez was out for blood. She couldn't picture her so-straitlaced stepbrother doing something so dangerous. Micah wasn't the sort of man who got involved in violence of any sort. Certainly, he was a far cry from the two mercenaries who'd shut down Lopez's operation. Maybe he'd given the information to the feds for Cy and Eb. Yes, that could have happened, somehow. She remembered what he'd said about the danger to his family and she felt chilled all over again. She'd load that shotgun when she and Jack got home, she told herself firmly, and she'd shoot it if she had to. She would protect her stepfather with her last breath.

As she turned down the street and drove out of town, toward the adult day care center where Jack Steele stayed following his stroke, she wondered where Micah was going in such a hurry. He didn't spend a lot of time in the States. He hadn't for years. He must have been visiting Eb Scott or Cy Parks. She knew they were friends. Odd friends for a tame man like Micah, she pondered. Even if they ran cattle now, they'd been professional mercenaries in the past. She wondered what Micah could possibly have in common with such men.

She was so lost in thought that she didn't notice that she was being followed by a dark, late model car. It didn't really occur to her that anyone would think of harming her, despite her brief argument with Micah just now. She was a nonentity. She had short, dark hair and pale blue eyes, and a nice but unremarkable figure. She was simply ordinary. She never attracted attention from men, and Micah had found her totally resistible from the day they met. Why not? He could have any woman he wanted. She'd seen him with really beautiful women when she and her mother had first come to live with Jack Steele. Besides, there was the age thing. Callie was barely twenty-two. Micah was thirty-six. He didn't like adolescents. He'd said that to Callie, just after that disastrous encounter—among other things. Some of the things he'd said still made her blush. He'd compared her to her mother, and he hadn't been kind. Afterward, she'd been convinced that he was having an affair with her mother, who didn't deny it when Callie asked. It had tarnished him in her eyes and made her hostile. She still was. It was something she couldn't help. She'd idolized Micah until she saw him kissing her mother. It had killed something inside her, made her cold. She wondered if he'd been telling the truth when he said he hadn't seen her mother recently. It hurt to think of him with Anna.

She stopped at a crossroads, her eyes darting from one stop sign to another, looking for oncoming traffic. While she was engrossed in that activity, the car following her on the deserted road suddenly shot ahead and cut across in front of her, narrowly missing her front bumper.

She gasped and hit the brake, forgetting to depress the clutch at the same time. The engine died. She reached over frantically to lock the passenger door, and at the same time, three slim, dark, formidable-looking men surrounded her car. The taller of the three jerked open the driver's door and pulled her roughly out of the car.

She fought, but a hand with a handkerchief was clapped over her nose and mouth and she moaned as the chloroform hit her nostrils and knocked her out flat. As she was placed quickly into the back seat of the other car, another man climbed into her little car and moved it onto the side of the road. He joined his colleagues. The dark car turned around and accelerated back the way it had come, with Callie unconscious in the back seat.

Micah Steele roared away from the scene of his latest disagreement with Callie, his chiseled mouth a thin line above his square jaw. His big hands gripped the steering wheel with cold precision as he cursed his own lack of communication skills. He'd put her back up almost at once by being disparaging about the neat beige suit she was wearing with a plain white blouse. She never dressed to be noticed, only to be efficient. She was that, he had to admit. She was so unlike him. He seemed conservative in his dress and manner. It was a deception. He was unconventional to the core, while Callie could have written the book on proper behavior.

She hadn't believed him, about the danger she and her stepfather—his father—could find themselves in. Manuel Lopez wasn't the man to cross, and he wanted blood. He was going to go to the easiest target for that. He grimaced, thinking how vulnerable Callie would be in a desperate situation. She hated snakes, but he'd seen her go out of her way not to injure one. She was like that about everything. She was a sucker for a hard-luck story, an easy mark for a con artist. Her heart was as soft as wool, and she was sensitive; overly sensitive. He didn't like remembering how he'd hurt her in the past.

He did remember that he hadn't eaten anything since breakfast. He stopped to have a sandwich at a local fast-food joint. Then he drove himself back to the motel he was staying at. He'd been helping Eb Scott and Cy Parks get rid of Lopez's fledgling drug distribution center. Just nights ago, they'd shut down the whole operation and sent most of Lopez's people to jail. Lopez's high-tech equipment, all his vehicles, even the expensive tract of land they sat on, had been confiscated under the Rico statutes. And that didn't even include the massive shipment of marijuana that had also been taken away. Micah himself had tipped off the authorities to the largest shipment of cocaine in the history of south Texas, which the Coast Guard, with DEA support, had appropriated before it even got to the Mexican coast. Lopez wouldn't have to dig too deeply to know that Micah had cost him not only the multimillion-dollar shipment, but the respect of the cartel in Colombia as well. Lopez was in big trouble with his bosses. Micah Steele was the reason for that. Lopez couldn't get to Micah, but he could get to Micah's family because they were vulnerable. The knowledge of that scared him to death.

He took a shower and stretched out on the bed in a towel, his hands under his damp blond hair while he stared at the ceiling and wondered how he could keep an eye on Callie Kirby and Jack Steele without their knowing. A private bodyguard would stick out like a sore thumb in a small Texas community like Jacobsville. On the other hand, Micah couldn't do it himself without drawing Lopez's immediate retaliation. It was a difficult determination. He couldn't make himself go back to the Bahamas while he knew his father and Callie were in danger. On the other hand, he couldn't stay here. Living in a small town would drive him nuts, even if he had done it in the past, before he went off to medical school.

While he was worrying about what to do next, the telephone rang.

"Steele," he said on a yawn. He was tired.

"It's Eb," came the reply. "I just had a phone call from Rodrigo," he added, mentioning a Mexican national who'd gone undercover for them in Lopez's organization. He'd since been discovered and was now hiding out in Aruba.

"What's happened?" Micah asked with a feeling of dread knotting his stomach.

"He had some news from a friend of his cousin, a woman who knows Lopez. Have you seen Callie Kirby today?" Eb asked hesitantly.

"Yes," Micah said. "About two hours ago, just as she was leaving her office. Why?"

"Rodrigo said Lopez was going to snatch her. He sounded as if they meant to do it pretty soon. You might want to check on her."

"I went to see her. I warned her...!"

"You know Lopez," Eb reminded him somberly. "It won't do her any good even if she's armed. Lopez's men are professionals."

"I'll do some telephoning and get back to you," Micah said quickly, cursing his own lack of haste about safeguarding Callie. He hung up and phoned the adult day care center. Callie would surely be there by now. He could warn her...

But the woman who answered the phone said that Callie hadn't arrived yet. She was two hours late, and her stepfather was becoming anxious. Did Micah know where she was?

He avoided a direct answer and promised to phone her back. Then, with a feeling of utter dread, he climbed into the Porsche and drove past Kemp's law office, taking the route Callie would have taken to the adult day care center.

His heart skipped a beat when he reached the first intersection outside the city. At this time of day, there was very little traffic. But there, on the side of the road, was Callie's yellow VW, parked on the grass with the driver's door wide-open.

He pulled in behind it and got out, cursing as he noted that the keys were still in the ignition, and her purse was lying on the passenger seat. There was no note, no anything.

He stood there, shell-shocked and cold. Lopez had Callie. Lopez had Callie!

After a minute, he phoned Eb on his car phone.

"What do you want me to do?" Eb asked at once, after Micah had finished speaking.

Micah's head was spinning. He couldn't think. He ran a hand through his thick hair. "Nothing. You're newly married, like Cy. I can't put any more women in the firing line. Let me handle this."

"What will you do?" Eb asked.

"Bojo's in Atlanta visiting his brother, but I'll have him meet me in Belize tomorrow. If you have a number for Rodrigo, call it, and tell him to meet me in Belize, too, at the Seasurfer's Bar. Meanwhile, I'll call in the rest of my team." He was remembering phone numbers and jotting them down even as he spoke. "They're taking a holiday, but I can round them up. I'll go in after her."

Eb suggested calling the chief of police, Chet Blake, because he had contacts everywhere, including relatives in positions of power—one was even a Texas Ranger. Micah couldn't argue. If Eb wanted to tell the man, let him. He was going to get to Callie while she was still alive.

"Just remember that somebody in law enforcement is feeding information to Lopez, and act accordingly. I've got to make arrangements about Dad before I leave.''

"I'm sorry, Micah.''

"It's my fault," Micah ground out furiously. "I shouldn't have left her alone for a minute! I warned her, but what good did that do?''

"Stop that," Eb said at once. "You're no good to Callie unless you can think straight. If you need any sort of help, logistical or otherwise, I have contacts of my own in Mexico.''

"I'll need ordinance," Micah said at once. "Can you set it up with your man in Belize and arrange to have him meet us at that border café we used to use for a staging ground?''

"I can. Tell me what you want.''

Micah outlined the equipment he wanted, including an old DC-3 to get them into the Yucatán, from which his men would drop with parachutes at night.

"You can fly in under the radar in that," Eb cautioned, "but the DEA will assume you're trying to bring in drugs if they spot you. It'll be tricky.''

"Damn!" Micah was remembering that someone in federal authority was on Lopez's payroll. "I had a contact near Lopez, but he left the country. Rodrigo's cousin might help, but he'd be risking his life after this latest tip he fed Rodrigo. So, basically, we've got nobody in Lopez's organization. And if I use my regular contacts, I risk alerting the DEA. Who can I trust?''

"I know someone," Eb said after a minute. "I'll take care of that. Phone me when you're on the ground in Cancún and make sure you've got global positioning equipment with you.''

"Will do. Thanks, Eb."

"What are friends for? I'll be in touch. Good luck."

"Thanks."

"Want me to call Cy?"

"No. I'll go by his place on my way out of town and catch him up." He hung up.

He didn't want to leave Callie's car with the door open and her purse in it, but he didn't want to be accused of tampering with evidence later. He compromised by locking it and closing the door. The police would find it eventually, because they patrolled this way. They'd take it from there, but he didn't want anyone in authority to know he was going after Callie. Someone had warned Lopez about the recent devastating DEA raid on his property. That person was still around, and Micah didn't want anyone to guess that he knew about Callie's kidnapping.

It was hard to think clearly, but he had to. He knew that Callie had a cell phone. He didn't know if she had it with her. Kemp, her boss, had let that slip to Eb Scott during a casual conversation. If Callie had the phone, and Lopez's people didn't know, she might be able to get a call out. He didn't flatter himself that she'd call him. But she might try to call the adult day care center, if she could. It wasn't much, but it gave him hope.

He drove to the center. For one mad instant he thought about speaking to his father in person. But that would only complicate matters and upset the old man; they hadn't spoken in years. He couldn't risk causing his father to have another stroke or a second

heart attack by telling him that Callie had been kidnapped.

He went to the office of the nursing director of the
center instead and took her into his confidence. She
agreed with him that it might be best if they kept the
news from his father, and they formulated a cover
story that was convincing. It was easy enough for
him to arrange for a nurse to go home with his father
to Callie's apartment every night and to drive him to
the center each day. They decided to tell Jack Steele
that one of Callie's elderly aunts had been hurt in a
car wreck and she had to go to Houston to see about
her. Callie had no elderly aunts, but Jack wouldn't
know that. It would placate him and keep him from
worrying. Then Micah would have to arrange for
someone to protect him from any attempts by Lopez
on his life.

He went back to his motel and spent the rest of
the night and part of the next day making international phone calls. He knew that Chet Blake, the police chief, would call in the FBI once Callie's disappearance was noted, and that wasn't a bad idea.
They would, of course, try to notify Micah, but they
wouldn't be able to find him. That meant that Lopez's man in law enforcement would think Micah
didn't know that his stepsister had been kidnapped.
And that would work to his benefit.

But if Lopez's men carried Callie down to the Yucatán, near Cancún, which was where the drug lord
lived these days, it was going to become a nightmare
of diplomacy for any U.S. agency that tried to get
her out of his clutches, despite international law enforcement cooperation. Micah didn't have that problem. He had Bojo, one of his best mercenaries, with

him in the States. It took time to track down the rest
of his team, but by dawn he'd managed it and arranged to meet them in Belize that night. He hated
waiting that long, and he worried about what Callie
was going to endure in the meantime. But any sort
of assault took planning, especially on a fortress like
Lopez's home. To approach it by sea was impossible.
Lopez had several fast boats and guards patrolling
the sea wall night and day. It would have to be a
land-based attack, which was where the DC-3 came
in. The trusty old planes were practically indestructible.

He couldn't get Callie's ordeal out of his mind.
He'd kept tabs on her for years without her knowledge. She'd dated one out-of-town auditor and a
young deputy sheriff, but nothing came of either relationship. She seemed to balk at close contact with
men. That was disturbing to him, because he'd made
some nasty allegations about her morals being as
loose as her mother's after she'd come on to him
under the mistletoe four years ago.

He didn't think words would be damaging, but
perhaps they were. Callie had a reputation locally for
being as pure as fresh snow. In a small town, where
everybody knew everything about their neighbors,
you couldn't hide a scandal. That made him feel even
more guilty, because Callie had been sweet and uninhibited until he'd gone to work on her. It was a
shame that he'd taken out his rage on her, when it
was her mother who'd caused all the problems in his
family. Callie's innocence was going to cost her
dearly, in Lopez's grasp. Micah groaned aloud as he
began to imagine what might happen to her now.
And it would be his fault.

He packed his suitcase and checked out of the motel. On the way to the airport, he went by Cy Parks's place, to tell him what was going on. Eb was doing enough already; Micah hated the thought of putting more on him. Besides, Cy would have been miffed if he was left out of this. He had his own reasons for wanting Lopez brought down. The vengeful drug lord had endangered the life of Cy's bride, Lisa, and the taciturn rancher wouldn't rest easy until Lopez got what was coming to him. He sympathized with Micah about Callie's kidnapping and Jack Steele's danger. To Micah's relief, he also volunteered to have one of his men, a former law enforcement officer, keep a covert eye on his father, just in case. That relieved Micah's troubled mind. He drove to the airport, left the rented Porsche in the parking lot with the attendant, and boarded the plane to Belize. Then he went to work.

Callie came to in a limousine. She was trussed up like a calf in a bulldogging competition, wrists and ankles bound, and a gag in her mouth. The three men who'd kidnapped her were conversing.

They weren't speaking Spanish. She heard at least one Arabic word that she understood. At once, she knew that they were Manuel Lopez's men, and that Micah had told the truth about the danger she and Jack were in. It was too late now, though. She'd been careless and she'd been snatched.

She lowered her eyelids when one of the men glanced toward her, pretending to still be groggy, hoping for a chance to escape. Bound as she was, that seemed impossible. She shifted a little, noticing with comfort the feel of the tiny cell phone she'd slipped into her slacks' pocket before leaving the office. If they didn't frisk her, she might get a call out. She remembered what she'd heard about Lopez, and her blood ran cold.

She couldn't drag her wrists out of the bonds. They felt like ropes, not handcuffs. Her arm was sore—she wondered if perhaps they'd given her a shot, a sedative of some sort. She must have been out a very long time. It had been late afternoon when she'd been kidnapped. Now it was almost dawn. She wished she had a drink of water....

The big limousine ate up the miles. She had some vague sensation that she'd been on an airplane. Perhaps they'd flown to an airport and the car had picked them up. If only she could see out the window. There were undefined shadows out there. They looked like trees, a lot of trees. Her vision was slightly blurred and she felt as if her limbs were made of iron. It was difficult to concentrate, and more difficult to try to move. What had they given her?

One man spoke urgently to the other and indicated Callie. He smiled and replied with a low, deep chuckle.

Callie noticed then that her blouse had come apart in the struggle. Her bra was visible, and those men were staring at her as if they had every right. She felt sick to her soul. It didn't take knowing the language to figure out what they were saying. She was completely innocent, but before this ordeal was over, she knew she never would be again. She felt a wave of grief wash over her. If only Micah hadn't pushed her away that Christmas. Now it was too late. Her first and last experience of men was going to be a nightmarish one, if she even lived through it. That seemed doubtful. Once the drug lord discovered that Micah had no affection for his stepsister, that he actually hated her and wouldn't soil his hands paying her ransom, she was going to be killed. She knew what happened in kidnappings. Most people knew. It had never occurred to her that she would ever figure in one. How ironic, that she was poor and unattractive, and that hadn't spared her this experience.

She wondered dimly what Micah would say when he knew she was missing. He'd probably feel well rid of her, but he might pay the ransom for her father's sake. Someone had to look after Jack Steele, something his only child couldn't apparently be bothered to do. Callie loved the old man and would have gladly sacrificed her life for him. That made her valuable in at least one way.

The one bright spot in all this was that once word of Callie's kidnapping got out, Micah would hire a bodyguard for Jack whether he wanted one or not. Jack would be safe.

She wished she knew some sort of self-defense, some way of protecting herself, of getting loose from the ropes and the gag that was slowly strangling her. She hadn't had time for lunch the day before and she'd been drugged for the whole night and into the next morning. She was sick and weak from hunger and thirst, and she really had to go to the bathroom. It was a bad day all around.

She closed her eyes and wished she'd locked her car doors and sped out of reach of her assailants. If there was a next time, if she lived to repeat her mistakes, she'd never repeat that one.

She shifted because her legs were cramping and she felt even sicker.

Listening to the men converse in Arabic, she realized her abductors weren't from Mexico. But as she looked out the window now, she could see the long narrow paved ribbon of road running through what looked like rain forest. She'd never been to the Yucatán, but she knew what it looked like from volumes of books she'd collected on Maya relics. Her heart sank. She knew that Manuel Lopez lived near Cancún, and she knew she was in the Yucatán. Her worst fears were realized.

Only minutes later, the car pulled into a long paved driveway through tall steel gates. The gates closed behind them. They sped up to an impressive whitewashed beach house overlooking a rocky bay. It had red ceramic tiles and the grounds were immaculate and full of blooming flowers. Hibiscus in November. She could have laughed hysterically. Back home the trees were bare, and here everything was blooming. She wondered what sort of fertilizer they used to grow those hibiscus flowers so big, and then she remembered Lopez's recent body count. She wondered if she might end up planted in his garden...

The car stopped. The door was opened by a suited dark man holding an automatic rifle of some sort, one of those little snub-nosed machine guns that crooks on television always seemed to carry.

She winced as the men dragged her out of the car and frog-marched her, bonds and all, into the ceramic tile floored lobby. The tile was black and white, like a chessboard. There was a long, graceful staircase and, overhead, a crystal chandelier that looked like

Waterford crystal. It probably cost two or three times the price of her car.

As she searched her surroundings, a small middle-aged man strolled out of the living room with his hands in his pockets. He didn't smile. He walked around Callie as if she were some sort of curiosity, his full lips pursed, his small dark eyes narrow and smugly gleaming. He jerked her gag down.

"Miss Kirby," he murmured in accented English. "Welcome to my home. I am Manuel Lopez. You will be my guest until your interfering stepbrother tries to rescue you," he added, hesitating in front of her. "And when he arrives, I will give him what my men have left of you, before I kill him, too!"

Callie thought that she'd never seen such cruelty in a human being's eyes in her life. The man made her knees shake. He was looking at her with contempt and possession. He reached out a stubby hand and ripped her blouse down in front, baring her small breasts in their cotton bra.

"I had expected a more attractive woman," he said. "Sadly you have no attractions with which to bargain, have you? Small breasts and a body that would afford little satisfaction. But Kalid likes women," he mused, glancing at the small, dark man who'd been sitting across from Callie. "When I need information, he is the man who obtains it for me. And although I need no information from you, Miss Kirby," he murmured, "it will please Kalid to practice his skills."

A rapid-fire burst of a guttural language met the statement.

"Español!" Lopez snapped. "You know I do not understand Arabic!"

"The woman," one of the other men replied in Spanish. "Before you give her to Kalid, let us have her."

Lopez glanced at the two thin, unshaven men who'd delivered Callie to him and smiled. "Why not? I make you a present of her. It should arouse even more guilt in her stepbrother to find her...used. But not until I tell you," he added coldly. "For now, take her to the empty servant's room upstairs. And put the gag back in place," he added. "I have important guests arriving. I would not want them to be disturbed by any unexpected noise."

"My stepbrother won't come to rescue me," she said hoarsely, shocked. "He isn't a physical sort of man. Aren't you going to ask him to pay ransom?"

Lopez looked at her as if she were nuts. "Why do you think Steele will not come after you?"

"He's a doctor. Or he was studying to be one. He wouldn't know the first thing about rescuing somebody!"

Lopez seemed to find that amusing.

"Besides that," she added harshly, "he hates me. He'll probably laugh his head off when he knows you've got me. He can't stand the sight of me."

That seemed to disturb Lopez, but after a minute he shrugged. *"No importa,"* he said lightly. "If he comes, that will be good. If not, it will make him even more concerned for his father. Who will be," he added with a cold smile, "next to feel my wrath."

Callie had her mouth open to ask another question, but at a signal from Lopez she was half dragged out of the room, her pale blue eyes as wide as saucers as she shivered with fear.

## Chapter Two

Callie had never been in such danger in her life, although she certainly knew what it was to be manhandled. She'd been in and out of foster care since the age of six. On a rare visit home, one of her mother's lovers had broken her arm when she was thirteen, after trying to fondle her. She'd run from him in horror, and he'd caught up with her at the staircase. A rough scuffle with the man had sent her tumbling down the steps to lie sprawled at the foot of the staircase.

Her mother had been furious, but not at her boyfriend, who said that Callie had called him names and threatened to tell her mother lies about him. After her broken arm had been set in a cast, Anna had taken Callie right back to her foster home, making her out to be incorrigible and washing her hands of responsibility for her.

Oddly, it had been Jack Steele's insistence that he wanted the child that had pushed a reluctant Anna into taking her back, at the age of fifteen. Jack had won her over, a day at a time. When Micah was home for holidays, he'd taunted her, made his disapproval of her so noticeable that her first lesson in the Steele home was learning how to avoid Jack's grown son. She'd had a lot of practice at avoiding men by then, and a lot of emotional scars. Anna had found that amusing. Never much of a mother, she'd ignored Callie to such an extent that the only affection Callie ever got was from Jack.

She closed her eyes. Her own father had ripped her out of his arms when she was six and pushed her away when she begged to stay with him. She was some other man's bastard, he'd raged, and he wanted no part of her. She could get out with her tramp of a mother—whom he'd just caught in bed with a rich friend—and he never wanted to see either of them again. She'd loved her father. She never understood why he couldn't love her back. Well, he thought she wasn't his. She couldn't really blame him for feeling that way.

She was still sitting in a small bedroom that night, having been given nothing to eat or drink. She was weak with hunger and pain, because the bonds that held her wrists and ankles had chafed and all but cut off the circulation. She heard noise downstairs from time to time. Obviously Lopez's visitors had stayed a long time, and been quite entertained, from the sound of things. She could hear the soft whisper of the ocean teasing the shore outside the window. She wondered what they would do with her body, after they killed her. Perhaps they'd throw her out there, to be eaten by sharks.

While she was agonizing over her fate, the sky had darkened. Hours more passed, during which she dozed a little. Then suddenly, she was alone no longer. The door opened and closed. She opened her tired eyes and saw the three men who'd kidnapped her, gathered around her like a pack of dogs with a helpless cat. One of them started stripping her while the others watched. Her cell phone fell out of the pocket of her slacks as they were pulled off her long legs. One of the men tossed it up and laughed, speaking to another man in yet a different foreign language.

Callie closed her eyes, shivering with fear, and prayed for strength to bear what was coming. She wished with all her heart that Micah hadn't pushed her away that last Christmas they'd spent together. Better him than any one of these cold, cruel, mocking strangers.

She heard one of them speaking in rough Spanish, discussing her body, making fun of her small breasts. It was like a playback from one foster home when she was fifteen, where an older son of the family had almost raped her before he was interrupted by the return of his parents. She'd run away afterward, and been sent to another foster home. She'd been saved that time, but she could expect no help now. Micah wouldn't begin to know how to rescue her, even if he was inclined to save her. He probably wouldn't consider ransom, either. She was alone in the world, with no one who would care about her fate. Her mother probably wouldn't even be bothered if she died. Like Micah, she'd blamed Callie for what had happened.

Desperate for some way to endure the ordeal, to block it out, Callie pictured the last time she'd seen her grandmother before she passed away, standing in an arbor of little pink fairy roses, waving. Callie had often stayed with her father's widowed mother when he and Anna were traveling. It was a haven of love. It hadn't lasted. Her grandmother had died suddenly when she was five. Everyone she'd ever loved had left her, in one way or the other. Nobody would even miss her. Maybe Jack would. She spared one last thought for the poor old man who was as alone as she was. But with her out of the way, perhaps Micah would go home again...

There was a loud, harsh shout. She heard the door open, and the men leave. With a shivery sigh, she moved backward until she could ease down into a worn wing chair by the fireplace. It wasn't going to be a long reprieve, she knew. If only she could free herself! But the bonds were cutting into her wrists and ankles. She was left in only a pair of aged white briefs and a tattered white bra, worn for comfort and not for appearance. No one had seen her in her underwear since she was a small child. She felt tears sting her eyes as she sat there, vulnerable and sick and ashamed. Any minute now, those men would be back. They would untie her before they used her. She knew that. She had to try to catch them off guard the instant she was free and run. If she could get into the jungle, she might have a chance. She was a fast sprinter, and she knew woodcraft. It was the last desperate hope she had.

One of the men, the one who'd asked Lopez for

her, came back inside for a minute, staring at her. He pulled out a wicked looking little knife and flicked it at one shoulder strap of her bra, cutting right through it.

She called him a foul name in Spanish, making herself understood despite the gag. Her mind raced along. If she could make him angry enough to free her, which he'd have to do if he had rape in mind... She repeated the foul name, with more fervor.

He cursed. But instead of pulling her up to untie her, he caught her by the shoulder and pressed her hard back into the chair, easing the point of the knife against the soft, delicate upper part of her breast.

She moaned hoarsely as the knife lightly grazed her flesh.

"You will learn manners before we finish with you," he drawled icily, in rough Spanish. "You will do what I tell you!"

He made no move to free her. Instead, he jerked down the side of her bra that had been cut, and stared mockingly at her breast.

The prick from the knife stung. She ground her teeth together. What had she been thinking? He wasn't going to free her. He was going to torture her! She felt sick unto death with fear as she looked up into his eyes and realized that he was enjoying both her shame and her fear.

In fact, he laughed. He went back and locked the door. "We don't need to be disturbed, do we?" he purred as he walked back toward her, brandishing the sharp knife. "I have looked forward to this all the way from Texas..."

Her eyes closed. She said a last, silent prayer. She

thought of Micah, and of Jack. Her chin lifted as she waited bravely for the impact of the blade.

There was a commotion downstairs and a commotion outside. She'd hoped it might divert the man standing over her with that knife, but he was too intent on her vulnerable state to care what was going on elsewhere. He put one hand on the back of the chair, beside her head, and placed the point of the knife right against her breast.

"Beg me not to do it," he chuckled. "Come on. Beg me."

Her terrified eyes met his and she knew that he was going to violate her. It was in his face. He was almost drooling with pleasure. She was cold all over, sick, resigned. She would die, eventually. But in the meantime, she was going to suffer a fate that would make death welcome.

"Beg me!" he demanded, his eyes flashing angrily, and the blade pushed harder.

There was a sudden burst of gunfire from somewhere toward the front of the house. Simultaneously, there was shattering glass behind the man threatening her, and the sudden audible sound of bullets hitting flesh. The man with the knife groaned once and fell into a silent, red-stained heap at her feet.

Wide-eyed, terrified, shaking, Callie cried out as she looked up into a face completely covered with a black mask, except for slits that bared a little of his eyes and mouth. He was dressed all in black with a wicked looking little machine gun in one hand and a huge knife suddenly in the other. His eyes went to her nicked breast. He made a rough sound and kicked the man on the floor aside as he pulled Callie up out of the chair and cut the bonds at her ankles and wrists.

Her hands and feet were asleep. She almost fell. He didn't even stop to unfasten the gag. Without a word, he bent and lifted her over his shoulder in the classic fireman's carry, and walked straight toward the window. Apparently, he was going out it, with her.

He finished clearing away the broken glass around the window frame and pulled a long black cord toward him. It seemed to be hanging from the roof.

He was huge and very strong. Callie, still in shock from her most recent ordeal, her feet and hands almost numb, didn't try to talk. She didn't even protest. If this was a turf war, and she was being stolen by another drug lord, perhaps he'd just hold her for ransom and not let his men torture her. She had little to say about her own fate. She closed her eyes and noticed that there was a familiar smell about the man who was abducting her. Odd. He must be wearing some cologne that reminded her of Jack, or even Mr. Kemp. At least he'd saved her from the knife.

Her wounded breast hurt, where it was pressed against the ribbed fabric of his long-sleeved shirt, and the small cut was bleeding slightly, but that didn't seem to matter. As long as he got her out of Lopez's clutches, she didn't really care what happened to her anymore. She was exhausted.

With her still over his shoulder, he stepped out onto the ledge, grasped a thick black cord in a gloved hand and, with his rifle leveled and facing forward, he rappelled right out the second-story window and down to the ground with Callie on his shoulder. She gasped as she felt the first seconds of free fall, and her hands clung to his shirt, but he didn't drop her. He seemed quite adept at rappelling.

She'd read about the Australian rappel, where men went down the rope face-front with a weapon in one hand. She'd never seen it done, except on television and in adventure movies. She'd never seen anyone doing it with a hostage over one shoulder. This man was very skillful. She wondered if he really was a rival drug lord, or if perhaps he was one of Eb Scott's mercenaries. Was it possible that Micah would have cared enough to ask Eb to mount her rescue? Her heart leaped at the possibility.

As they reached the ground, she realized that her rescuer wasn't alone. As soon as they were on the ground, he made some sort of signal with one hand, and men dressed in black, barely visible in the security lights dotted along the dark estate, scattered to the winds. Men in suits, still firing after them, began to run toward the jungle.

A four-wheel-drive vehicle was sitting in the driveway with its engine running and the back seat door open, waiting.

Her rescuer threw her inside, climbed in beside her and slammed the door. She pulled the gag off.

"Hit it!" he bit off.

The vehicle spun dirt and gravel as it took off toward the gate. The windows were open. Gunfire hit the side of the door, and was returned by the man sitting beside Callie and the man in the front passenger seat. The other armed man had a slight, neatly trimmed beard and mustache and he looked as formidable as his comrade. The man who was driving handled the vehicle expertly, dodging bullets even as his companions returned fire at the pursuing vehicle.

Callie had seen other armed men in black running for the jungle. She revised her opinion that these were rival drug dealers. From the look of these men, they were commandos. She assumed that these three men were part of some sort of covert group sent in to rescue her. Only one person would have the money to mount such an expedition, and she'd have bet money that Eb Scott was behind it somehow. Micah must have paid him to hire these men to come after her.

If he had, she was grateful for his intervention, although she wondered what had prompted it. Perhaps his father had persuaded him. God knew, he'd never have spent that sort of money on her rescue for his own sake. Her sudden disappearance out of his life would have delighted him.

She was chilled and embarrassed, sitting in her underwear with three strange men, but her clothing had been ripped beyond repair. In fact, her rescuer hadn't even stopped to grab it up on his way out of the room where she was being held. She made herself as inconspicuous as possible, grateful that there was no light inside the vehicle, and closed her eyes while the sound of gunfire ricocheted around her. She didn't say a word. Her companions seemed quite capable of handling this new emergency. She wasn't going to distract them. If she caught a stray bullet, that was all right, too. Anything, even death, would be preferable to what she would endure if Lopez regained custody of her.

Half a mile down the road, there was a deep curve. The big man who'd rescued Callie told the man in front to stop the vehicle. He grabbed a backpack on the floorboard, jumped out, pulled Callie out, and motioned the driver and the man with the beard and mustache to keep going. The big man carried Callie out of sight of the road and dashed her down in the dark jungle undergrowth, his powerful body lying alongside hers in dead leaves and debris while they waited for the Jeep that had been chasing them to appear. Thorns dug into her bare arms and legs, but she was so afraid that she hardly noticed.

Suddenly, the pursuing Jeep came into sight. It braked for the curve, but it barely slowed down as it shot along after the other vehicle. Its taillights vanished around the bend. So far, so good, Callie thought, feeling oddly safe with the warmth and strength of the man lying so close beside her. But she hoped the man who was driving their vehicle and his bearded companion made a clean getaway. She wouldn't want them shot, even to save herself.

"That went well," her companion murmured curtly, rising. He pulled out some sort of electronic gadget and pushed buttons. He turned, sighting along it. "Can you walk?" he asked Callie.

His voice was familiar. Her mind must be playing tricks. She stood up, still in her underwear and barefoot.

"Yes. But I...don't have any shoes," she said hoarsely, still half in shock.

He looked down at her, aiming a tiny flashlight at her body, and a curse escaped his mouth as he saw her mangled bra.

"What the hell did they do to you?" he asked through his teeth.

Amazing, how familiar that deep voice was. "Not as much as they planned to, thanks to you," she said, trying to remain calm. "It's not a bad cut, just a graze. I'll have to have some sort of shoes if we're going to walk. And I...I don't suppose you have an extra shirt?'' she added with painful dignity.

He was holding a backpack. He pulled out a big black T-shirt and stuffed her into it. He had a pair of camouflage pants, too. They had to be rolled up, but they fit uncannily well. His face was solemn as he dug into the bag a second time and pulled out a pair of leather loafers and two pairs of socks.

''They'll be too big, but the socks will help them fit. They'll help protect your feet. Hurry. Lopez's men are everywhere and we have a rendezvous to make.''

She felt more secure in the T-shirt and camouflage pants. Not wanting to hold him up, she slipped quickly into the two pairs of thick socks and rammed her feet into the shoes. It was dark, but her companion had his small light trained ahead. She noticed that huge knife in his left hand as he started ahead of her. She remembered that Micah was left-handed...

The jungle growth was thick, but passable. Her companion shifted his backpack, so dark that it blended in with his dark gear and the jungle.

''Stay close behind me. Don't speak unless I tell you to. Don't move unless I move.''

''Okay,'' she said in a husky whisper, without argument.

''When we get where we're going, I'll take care of that cut.''

She didn't answer him. She was exhausted. She was also dying of thirst and hunger, but she knew there wasn't time for the luxury of food. She concentrated on where she was putting her feet, and prayed that she wouldn't trip over a huge snake. She knew there were snakes and lizards and huge spiders in the jungle. She was afraid, but Lopez was much more terrorizing a threat than a lonesome snake.

She followed her taciturn companion through the jungle growth, her eyes restless, her ears listening for any mechanical sound. The darkness was oddly comforting, because sound traveled so well in it. Once, she heard a quick, sharp rustle of the underbrush and stilled, but her companion quickly trained his light on it. It was only an iguana.

She laughed with delight at the unexpected encounter, bringing a curt jerk of the head from her companion, who seemed to find her amusement odd. He didn't say anything, though. He glanced at his instrument again, stopped to listen and look, and started off again.

Thorns in some of the undergrowth tore at her bare arms and legs, and her face. She didn't complain. Remembering where she'd been just before she was rescued made her grateful for any sort of escape, no matter how physically painful it might be.

She began to make a mental list of things she had to do when they reached safety. First on the list was to phone and see if Jack Steele was all right. He must be worried about her sudden disappearance. She didn't want him to suffer a setback.

Her lack of conversation seemed to puzzle the big man leading her through the jungle. He glanced back at her frequently, presumably to make sure she was behind him, but he didn't speak. He made odd movements, sometimes doubling back on the trail he made, sometimes deliberately snapping twigs and stepping on grass in directions they didn't go. Callie just followed along mindlessly.

At least two hours passed before he stopped, near a small stream. "We should be safe enough here for the time being," he remarked as he put down the backpack and opened it, producing a small bottle of water. He tossed it to Callie. "I imagine you're thirsty."

She opened it with trembling hands and swallowed half of it down at once, tears stinging her eyes at the pleasure of the wetness on her tongue, in her dry mouth.

He set up a small, self-contained light source, revealing his companion. He moved closer, frowning at her enthusiastic swallowing as he drew a first aid kit from his backpack. "When did you last have anything to drink?" he asked softly.

"Day…before yesterday," she choked.

He cursed. In the same instant, he pulled off the mask he'd been wearing, and Callie dropped the water bottle as her eyes encountered the dark ones of her stepbrother, Micah, in the dim light.

He picked up the water bottle and handed it back to her. "I thought it might come as a shock," he said grimly, noting her expression.

"You came after me yourself?" she asked, aghast. "But, how? Why?"

"Lopez has an agent in one of the federal agencies," he told her flatly. "I don't know who it is. I couldn't risk letting them come down here looking for you and having someone sell you out before I got here. Not that it would have been anytime soon. They're probably still arguing over jurisdictions as we speak." He pulled out a foil-sealed package and tossed it to her. "It's the equivalent of an MRE—a meal ready to eat. Nothing fancy, but if you're hungry, you won't mind the taste.''

"Thanks,'' she said huskily, tearing into it with urgent fingers that trembled with hunger.

He watched her eat ravenously, and he scowled. "No food, either?''

She shook her head. "You don't feed people you're going to kill,'' she mumbled through bites of chicken and rice that tasted freshly cooked, if cold.

He was very still. "Excuse me?''

She glanced at him while she chewed a cube of chicken. "He gave me to three of his men and told them to kill me.'' She swallowed and averted her eyes. "He said they could do whatever they liked to me first. So they did. At least, they started to, when you showed up. I was briefly alone with a smaller man, Arabic I think, and I tried to make him mad enough to release me so I had one last chance at escape. It made him mad, all right, but instead of untying me, he...put his knife into me.'' She chewed another cube of chicken, trying not to break down. "He said it was a...a taste of what to expect if I resisted him again. When you came in through the window, he was just about to violate me.''

"I'm going to take care of that cut right now. Infection sets in fast in tropical areas like this.'' He opened the first-aid box and checked through his supplies. He muttered something under his breath.

He took the half-finished meal away from her and stripped her out of the T-shirt. She grimaced and lowered her eyes as her mutilated bra and her bare breast were revealed, but she didn't protest.

"I know this is going to be hard for you, considering what you've just been through. But try to remember that I'm a doctor," he said curtly. "As near as not, anyway."

She swallowed, her eyes still closed tight. "At least you won't make fun of my body while you're working on it," she said miserably.

He was opening a small bottle. "What's that?"

"Nothing," she said wearily. "Oh God, I'm so tired!"

"I can imagine."

She felt his big, warm hands reach behind her to unfasten the bra and she caught it involuntarily.

He glanced at her face in the small circle of light from the lantern. "If there was another way, I'd take it."

She drew in a slow breath and closed her eyes, letting go of the fabric. She bit her lip and didn't look as he peeled the fabric away from her small, firm breasts.

The sight of the small cut made him furious. She had pretty little breasts, tip-tilted, with dusky nipples. He could feel himself responding to the sight of her, and he had to bite down hard on a wave of desire.

He forced himself to focus on the cut, and nothing else. The bra, he stuffed in his backpack. He didn't dare leave signs behind them. There wasn't much chance that they were closely followed, but he had to be careful.

He had to touch her breast to clean the small cut, and she jerked involuntarily.

"I won't hurt you any more than I have to," he promised quietly, mistaking her reaction for pain. "Grit your teeth."

She did, but it didn't help. She bit almost through her lip as he cleaned the wound. The sight of his big, lean hands on her body was breathtaking, arousing even under the circumstances. The pain was secondary to the hunger she felt for him, a hunger that had lasted for years. He didn't know, and she couldn't let him know. He hated her.

She closed her eyes while he put a soft bandage over the cleaned wound, taping it in place.

"God in heaven, I thought I'd seen every kind of lowlife on earth, but the guy who did this to you was a class all by himself," he growled.

She remembered the man and shuddered. Micah was pulling the shirt down over her bandaged breast. "It probably doesn't seem like it, but I got off lucky," she replied.

He looked into her eyes. "It's just a superficial wound so you won't need stitches. It probably won't even leave a scar there."

"It wouldn't matter," she said quietly.

"It would." He got up, drawing her up with him. "You're still nervous of me, after all this time."

She didn't meet his eyes. "You don't like me."

"Oh, for God's sake," he burst out, letting go of her shoulders. He turned away to deal with the medical kit. "Haven't you got eyes?"

She wondered what that meant. She was too tired to work it out. She sat down again and picked up her half-eaten meal, finishing it with relish. It was hard to look at him, after he'd seen her like that.

She fingered the rolled-up pair of camouflage pants she was wearing. "These aren't big enough to be yours," she remarked.

"They're Maddie's. She gave me those for you, and the shoes and socks, on the way out of Texas," he commented when he noticed her curious exploration of the pants.

He worked with some sort of electronic device.

"What's that thing?" she asked.

"GPS," he explained. "Global positioning. I can give my men a fix on our position, so they can get a chopper in here to pick us up and pinpoint our exact location. There's a clearing just through there where we'll rendezvous," he added, nodding toward the jungle.

Suddenly she frowned. "Who's Maddie?" she asked.

"Maddie's my scrounger. Anything we need on site that we didn't bring, Maddie can get. She's quite a girl. In fact," he added, "she looks a lot like you. She was mistaken for you at a wedding I went to recently in Washington, D.C."

That was disturbing. It sounded as though he and this Maddie were in partnership or something. She hated the jealousy she felt, when she had no right to be jealous. Old habits died hard.

"Is she here?" she asked, still puzzled by events and Micah's strange skills.

"No. We left her back in the States. She's working on some information I need, about the mole working for the feds, and getting some of your things together to send on to Miami."

She blinked. "You keep saying 'we,'" she pointed out.

His chin lifted. He studied her, unsmiling. "Exactly what do you think I do for a living, Callie?" In the dim light, his blond hair shone like muted moonlight. His handsome face was all angles and shadows. Her vision was still a little blurred from whatever the kidnapper had given her. So was her mind.

"Your mother left you a trust," she pointed out.

"My mother left me ten thousand dollars," he replied. "That wouldn't pay to replace the engine on the Ferrari I drive in Nassau."

Her hands stilled on the fork and tray. Some odd ideas were popping into her head. "You finished your residency?" she fished.

He shook his head. "Medicine wasn't for me."

"Then, what…?"

"Use your mind, Callie," he said finally, irritated. "How many men do you know who could rappel into a drug lord's lair and spirit out a hostage?"

Her breath caught. "You work for some federal agency?"

"Good God!" He got up, moved to his backpack and started repacking it. "You really don't have a clue, do you?"

"I don't know much about you, Micah," she confided quietly as she finished her meal and handed him the empty tray and fork. "That was the way you always wanted it."

"In some cases, it doesn't pay to advertise," he said carelessly. "I used to work with Eb Scott and Cy Parks, but now I have my own group. We hire out to various world governments for covert ops." He glanced at her stunned face. "I worked for the justice department for a couple of years, but now I'm a mercenary, Callie."

She was struck dumb for several long seconds. She swallowed. It explained a lot. "Does your father know?" she asked.

"He does not," he told her. "And I don't want

him to know. If he still gives a damn about me, it would only upset him.''

"He loves you very much," she said quietly, avoiding his angry black eyes. "He'd like to mend fences, but he doesn't know how. He feels guilty, for making you leave and blaming you for what…what my mother did.''

He pulled out a foil sealed meal for himself and opened it before he spoke. "You blamed me as well.''

She wrapped her arms around herself. It was cold in the jungle at night, just like they said in the movies. "Not really. My mother is very beautiful," she said, recalling the older woman's wavy jet-black hair and vivid blue eyes and pale skin. "She was a model just briefly, before she married my…her first husband.''

He frowned. "You were going to say, your father.''

She shivered. "He said I wasn't his child. He caught her in bed with some rich man when I was six. I didn't understand at the time, but he pushed me away pretty brutally and said not to come near him again. He said he didn't know whose child I was. That was when she put me in foster care.''

Micah stared at her, unspeaking, for several long seconds. "Put you in what?''

She swallowed. "She gave me up for adoption on the grounds that she couldn't support me. I went into a juvenile home, and from there to half a dozen foster homes. I only saw her once in all those years, when she took me home for Christmas. It didn't last long.'' She stared down at the jungle floor. "When she married your father, he wanted me, so she told him I'd been staying with my grandmother. I was in a foster home, but she got me out so she could convince your father that she was a good mother.'' She laughed hollowly. ''I hadn't seen her or heard from her in two years by then. She told me I'd better make a good job of pretending affection, or she'd tell the authorities I'd stolen something valuable—and instead of going back into foster care for two more years, I'd go to jail.''

## Chapter Three

Micah didn't say a word. He repacked the first-aid kit into his backpack with quick, angry movements. He didn't look at Callie.

"I guess you know how to use that gun," she said quietly. "If we're found, or if it looks like Lopez is going to catch us, I want you to shoot me. I'd rather die than face what you saved me from."

She said it in such a calm, quiet tone that it made all the more impact.

He looked up, scanning her drawn, white face in the soft light from the lantern. "He won't get you. I promise."

She drew a slow breath. "Thanks." She traced a fingernail over the camouflage pants. "And thanks for coming to get me. Lopez said he didn't have any plans to ransom me. He was going to let his men kill me because he thought it would make you suffer."

"What did you tell him?"

"That you were my worst enemy and you wouldn't care if he killed me," she said carelessly. "But he said you did care about your father, and he was the next victim. I hope you've got someone watching Dad," she added fervently. "If anything happens to him…!"

"You really love him, don't you?" he asked in an odd tone.

"He's the only person in my whole life who ever loved me," she said in a strained whisper.

A harsh sound broke from his lips. He got up and started getting things together. He pulled out what looked like a modified cell phone and spoke into it. A minute later, he put it back into the backpack.

"They're on the way in." He stood over her, his face grim as he picked up the small lantern and extinguished the light. "I know you must be cold. I'm sorry. I planned a quick airlift, so I didn't pack for a prolonged trek."

"It's all right," she said at once. "Cold is better than tortured."

He cursed under his breath as he hefted the backpack. "We have to get to that small clearing on the other side of the stream. It isn't deep, but I can carry you…"

"I'll walk," she said with quiet dignity, standing up. It was still painful to move, because she'd been tied up for so long, but she didn't let on. "You've done enough already."

"I've done nothing," he spat. He turned on his heel and led the way to the bank of the small stream, offering a hand.

She didn't take it. She knew he found her repulsive. He'd even told her mother that. She'd enjoyed taunting Callie with it. Callie had never understood why her mother hated her so much. Perhaps it was because she wasn't pretty.

"Walk where I do," he bit off as he dropped his hand. "The rocks will be slippery. Go around them, not over them."

"Okay."

He glanced over his shoulder as they started over the shallow stream. "You're damned calm for someone who's been through what you have in the past two days."

She only smiled. "You have no idea what I've been through in my life."

He averted his eyes. It was as if he couldn't bear to look at her anymore. He picked his way across to the other bank. Callie followed obediently, her feet cold and wet, her body shivering. Only a little longer, she told herself, and she would be home with Jack. She would be completely safe. Except...Lopez was still out there. She shivered again.

"Cold?" he asked when they were across.

"I'll be fine," she assured him.

He led her through one final tangle of brush, which he cut out of the way with the knife. She could see the silver ripple of the long blade in the dim light of the small flashlight he carried. She put one foot in front of the other and tried to blank out what would happen if Lopez's men caught up with them. It was terrifying.

They made it to the clearing just as a dark, noisy silhouette dropped from the sky and a door opened.

"They spotted us on radar!" came a loud voice

from the chopper. "They'll be here in two minutes. Run!"

"Run as if your life depended on it!" Micah told Callie, giving her a push.

She did run, her mind so affected by what she'd already endured that she almost kept up with her long-legged stepbrother. He leaped right up into the chopper and gave her a hand up. She landed in a heap on the dirty floor, and laughed with relief.

The door closed and the chopper lifted. Outside, there were sounds like firecrackers in the wake of the noise the propellers made. Gunfire, Callie knew.

"It always sounds like firecrackers in real life," she murmured. "It doesn't sound that way in the movies."

"They augment the sound in movies, mademoiselle." A gentle hand eased her into a seat on the edge of the firing line Micah and two other men made at the door.

She looked up. There was barely any light in the helicopter, but she could make out a beard and a mustache on a long, lean face. "You made it, too!" she exclaimed with visible relief. "Oh, I'm glad. I felt bad that you and the other man had to be decoys, just to get me out."

"It was no trouble, mademoiselle," the man said gently, smiling at her. "Rest now. They won't catch us. This is an Apache helicopter, one of the finest pieces of equipment your country makes. It has some age, but we find it quite reliable in tight situations."

"Is it yours?" she asked.

He laughed. "You might say that we have access to it, and various other aircraft, when we need them."

"Don't bore her to death, Bojo," a younger voice chuckled.

"Listen to him!" Bojo exclaimed. "And do you not drone on eternally about that small computer you carry, Peter, and its divine functions?"

A dark-haired, dark-eyed young man with white teeth came into view, a rifle slung over his shoulder. "Computers are my specialty," he said with a grin. "You're Callie? I'm Peter Stone. I'm from Brooklyn. That's Bojo, he's from Morocco. I guess you know Micah. And Smith over there—" he indicated a huge dark-eyed man "—runs a seafood restaurant in Charleston, along with our Maddie and a couple of guys we seem to have misplaced..."

"We haven't misplaced them," Micah said curtly. "They've gone ahead to get the DC-3 gassed up."

Bojo grinned. "Lopez will have men waiting at the airport for us."

"While we're taking off where we landed—at Laremos's private airstrip," Micah replied calmly. "And Laremos will have a small army at his airstrip, just in case Lopez does try anything."

"But what about customs?" Callie voiced.

Everybody laughed.

She flushed, realizing now that her captors hadn't gone through customs, and neither had these men. "Okay, I get it, but what about getting back into the States from here? I don't have a passport..."

"You have a birth certificate," Micah reminded her. "It'll be waiting in Miami, along with a small bag containing some of your own clothes and shoes. That's why Maddie didn't come with us," he added smugly.

"Miami?" she exclaimed, recalling belatedly that he'd mentioned that before. "Why not Texas?"

"You're coming back to the Bahamas with me, Callie," Micah replied. "You'll be Lopez's priority now. He'll be out for revenge, and it will take all of us to keep you safe."

She gaped at him. "But, Dad..." she groaned.

"Dad is in good hands. So are you. Now try not to worry. I know what I'm doing."

She bit her lower lip. None of this was making sense, and she was still scared, every time she thought about Lopez. But all these men surrounding her looked tough and battle-hardened, and she knew they wouldn't let her be recaptured.

"Who's Laremos?" Callie asked curiously, a minute later.

"He's retired now," Micah said, coming away from the door. "But he and 'Dutch' van Meer and J. D. Brettman were the guys who taught us the trade. They were the best. Laremos lives outside Cancún on a plantation with his wife and kids, and he's got the equivalent of a small army around him. Even the drug lords avoid his place. We'll get out all right, even if Lopez has his men tracking us."

She averted her eyes and folded her arms tightly around her body.

"You are shivering," Bojo said gently. "Here." He found a blanket and wrapped it around her.

That one simple act of compassion brought all her repressed fear and anguish to the surface. She bawled. Not a sound touched her lips. But tears poured from her eyes, draping themselves hot and wet across her pale cheeks and down to the corner of her pretty bow mouth.

Micah saw them and his face hardened like rock.

She turned her face toward the other side of the helicopter. She was used to hiding her tears. They mostly angered people, made them more hostile. Or they showed a weakness that was readily exploited. It was always better not to let people know they had the power to hurt you.

She wrapped the blanket closer and didn't speak the rest of the way. She closed her eyes, wiping at them with the blanket. Micah spoke in low tones to the other men, and although she couldn't understand what he was saying, she understood that rough, angry tone. She'd heard it enough at home.

For now, all she wanted to do was get to safety, to a place where Lopez and the animals who worked for him couldn't find her, couldn't hurt her. She was more afraid now than she had been on the way out of Texas, because now she knew what recapture would mean. The darkness was a friend in which she could hide her fear, conceal her terror. The sound of the propellers became suddenly like a mechanical lullaby in her ears, lulling her, like the whispers of the deep voices around her, into a brief, fitful sleep.

She felt an odd lightness in her stomach and opened her eyes to find the helicopter landing at what looked like a small airstrip on private land.

A big airplane, with scars and faded lettering, was waiting with its twin prop engines already running. Half a dozen armed men in camouflage uniforms stood with their guns ready to fire. A tall, imposing man with a mustache came forward. He had a Latin look about him, dark eyes and graceful movement.

He shook hands with Micah and spoke to him quietly, so that his voice didn't carry. Micah listened, and then nodded. They shook hands again. The man glanced at Callie curiously, and smiled in her direction.

She smiled back, her whole young face drawn and fatigued.

Micah motioned to her. "We have to get airborne before Lopez's men get here. Climb aboard. Thanks, Diego!" he called to the man.

*"No es nada,"* came the grinning reply.

"Was that the man you know, with the plantation?" Callie asked when they were inside and the door was closed.

"That was Laremos," he agreed.

"He and his family won't be hurt on our account, will they?" she persisted.

He glanced down at her. "No," he said slowly. His eyes searched hers until she looked away, made uneasy and shivery by the way he was looking at her.

He turned and made his way down the aisle to the cockpit. Two men poked their heads out of it, grinning, and after he spoke to them, they revved up the engines.

The passengers strapped themselves into their seats. Callie started to sit by herself, but Micah took her arm and guided her into the seat beside his. It surprised her, but she didn't protest. He reached across her to fasten her seat belt, bringing his hard, muscular chest pressing gently against her breasts.

She gasped as the pressure made the cut painful.

"God, I'm sorry! I forgot," he said, his hand going naturally, protectively, to her breast, to cup it gently. "Is it bad?"

She went scarlet. Of course, nobody was near

enough to see what was going on, but it embarrassed her to have him touch her with such familiarity. And then she remembered that he'd had her nude from the waist up on one side while he cleaned and bandaged that cut.

Her eyes searched his while she tried to speak. Her tongue felt swollen. Her breath came jerkily into her throat and her lips parted under its force. She felt winded, as if she'd fallen from a height.

His thumb soothed the soft flesh around the cut. "When we get to Miami, I'll take you to a friend of mine who's in private practice. We'll get you checked out before we fly out to the Bahamas."

His other arm, muscular and warm, was under her head. She could feel his breath, mint-scented and warm, on her lips as he searched her eyes.

His free hand left her breast and gently cupped her softly rounded chin. "Soft skin," he whispered deeply. "Soft heart. Sweet, soft mouth…"

His lips pressed the words against hers, probing tenderly. He caught her upper lip in both of his and tasted it with his tongue. Then he lifted away to look down into her shocked, curious eyes.

"You should hate me," he whispered. "I hurt you, and you did nothing, nothing at all to deserve it."

She winced, remembering how it had been when he'd lived with his father. "I understood. You resented me. My mother and I were interlopers."

"Your mother, maybe. Never you." He looked formidable, angry and bitter. But his black eyes were unreadable. "I've hesitated to ask. Maybe I don't really want to know. When Lopez had you," he began with uncharacteristic hesitation, "were you raped?"

"No," she said quietly. "But I was about to be. I remember thinking that if it hadn't all gone wrong that Christmas..." Her voice stopped. She was horrified at what she was about to say.

"I know," he interrupted, and he didn't smile. "I thought about it, too. What Lopez's damned henchmen did to you at least wouldn't have been your first experience of intimacy, if I hadn't acted like a prize heel with you!"

He seemed maddened by the knowledge. His hand on her face was hard and the pressure stung.

"Please," she whispered, tugging at his fingers.

He relaxed them at once. "I'm sorry," he bit off. "I'm still on edge. This whole thing has been a nightmare."

"Yes." She searched his black eyes, wishing she knew what he was thinking.

His thumb brushed softly over her swollen mouth. "Lopez will never get the chance to hurt you again," he said quietly. "I give you my word."

She bit her lower lip when his hand lifted away, shy of him. "Do you really think he'll come after me again?"

"I think he'll try," he said honestly.

She shivered, averting her eyes to the aisle beside them. "I hate remembering how helpless I was."

"I've been in similar situations," he said surprisingly. "Once I was captured on a mission and held for execution. I was tied up and tortured. I know how it feels."

She gaped at him, horrified. "How did you escape?"

"Bojo and the others came in after me," he said simply. "Under impossible odds, too." He smiled, and it was the first genuine smile he'd ever given her. "I guess they missed being yelled at."

She smiled back, hesitantly. It was new to relax with Micah, not to be on her guard against antagonistic and sarcastic comments.

He touched her face with a curious intensity in his eyes. "You must have been terrified when you were kidnapped. You've never known violence."

She didn't tell him, but she had, even if not as traumatically as she had at Lopez's. She lowered her gaze to his hard, disciplined mouth. "I never expected to be rescued at all, least of all by you. I wasn't even sure you'd agree to pay a ransom if they'd asked for one."

He scowled. "Why not?"

"You don't like me," she returned simply. "You never did."

He seemed disturbed. "It's a little more complicated than that, Callie."

"All the same, thank you for saving me," she continued. "You risked your own life to get me out."

"I've been risking it for years," he said absently while he studied her upturned face. She was too pale, and the fatigue she felt was visible. "Why don't you try to sleep? It's going to be a long flight."

Obviously he didn't want to talk. But she didn't mind. She was worn-out. "Okay," she agreed with a smile.

He moved back and she leaned her head back, closed her eyes, and the tension of the past two days caught up with her all at once. She fell asleep almost at once and didn't wake up until they were landing.

She opened her eyes to find a hard, warm pillow

under her head. To her amazement, she was lying across Micah's lap, with her cheek on his chest.

"Wakey, wakey," he teased gently. "We're on the ground."

"Where?" she asked, rubbing her eyes like a sleepy child.

"Miami."

"Oh. At the airport."

He chuckled. "*An* airport," he corrected. "But this one isn't on any map."

He lifted her gently back into her own seat and got to his feet, stretching hugely. He grinned down at her. "Come on, pilgrim. We've got a lot to do, and not much time."

She let him lead her off the plane. The other men had all preceded them, leaving behind automatic weapons, pistols and other paraphernalia.

"Aren't you forgetting your equipment?" she asked Micah.

He smiled and put a long finger against her mouth. His eyes were full of mischief. He'd never joked with her, not in all the years they'd known each other.

"It isn't ours," he said in a stage whisper. "And see that building, and those guys coming out of it?"

"Yes."

"No," he corrected. "There's no building, and those guys don't exist. All of this is a figment of your imagination, especially the airplane."

"My gosh!" she exclaimed with wide eyes. "We're working for the CIA?"

He burst out laughing. "Don't even ask me who they are. I swore I'd never tell. And I never will. Now let's go, before they get here."

He and the others moved rapidly toward a big

sport utility vehicle sitting just off the apron where they'd left the plane.

"Are you sure you cleared this with, uh—" Peter gave a quick glance at Callie "—the man who runs this place?"

"Eb did," Micah told him. "But just in case, let's get the hell out of Dodge, boys!"

He ran for the SUV, pushing Callie along. The others broke into a run as well, laughing as they went.

There was a shout behind them, but it was still hanging on the air when the driver, one of the guys in the cockpit, burned rubber taking off.

"He'll see the license plate!" Callie squeaked as she saw a suited man with a notepad looking after them.

"That's the idea," the young man named Peter told her with a grin. "It's a really neat plate, too. So is this vehicle. It belongs to the local director of the—" he hesitated "—of an agency we know. We, uh, had a friend borrow it from his house last night."

"We'll go to prison for years!" Callie exclaimed, horrified.

"Not really," the driver said, pulling quickly into a parking spot at a local supermarket. "Everybody out."

Callie's head was spinning. They got out of the SUV and into a beige sedan sitting next to it, with keys in the ignition. She was crowded into the back with Micah and young Peter, while the two pilots, one a Hispanic and the other almost as blond as Micah, crowded Bojo on either side in the front. The driver took off at a sedate pace and pulled out into Miami traffic.

That was when she noticed that all the men were wearing gloves. She wasn't. "Oh, that's lovely," she muttered. "That's just lovely! Everybody's wearing gloves but me. My fingerprints will be the only ones they find, and *I'll* go to prison for years. I guess you'll all come and visit me Sundays, right?" she added accusingly.

Micah chuckled with pure delight. "The guy who owns the SUV is a friend of Eb's, and even though he doesn't show it, he has a sense of humor. He'll double up laughing when he runs your prints and realizes who had his four-wheel drive. I'll explain it to you later. Take us straight to Dr. Candler's office, Don," he told the blond guy at the wheel. "You know where it is."

"You bet, boss," came the reply.

"I'm not going to prison?" Callie asked again, just to be sure.

Micah pursed his lips. "Well, that depends on whether or not the guy at customs recognizes us. I was kidding!" he added immediately when she looked ready to cry.

She moved her shoulder and grimaced. "I'll laugh enthusiastically when I get checked out," she promised.

"He'll take good care of you," Micah assured her. "He and I were at medical school together."

"Is he, I mean, does he do what you do?"

"Not Jerry," he told her. "He specializes in trauma medicine. He's chief of staff at a small hospital here."

"I see," she said, nodding. "He's a normal person."

Micah gave her a speaking glance while the others chuckled.

* * *

The hospital where Micah's friend worked was only a few minutes from the airport. Micah took Callie inside while the others waited in the car. Micah had a private word with the receptionist, who nodded and left her desk for a minute. She came back with a tall, dark-headed man about Micah's age. He motioned to Micah.

Callie was led back into an examination room. Micah sank into a chair by the desk.

"Are you going to sit there the whole time?" Callie asked Micah, aghast, when the doctor asked her to remove the shirt she was wearing so he could examine her.

"You haven't got anything that I haven't seen, and I need to explain to Jerry what I did to treat your wound." He proceeded to do that while Callie, uncomfortable and shy, turned her shoulder to him and removed the shirt.

After checking her vital signs, Dr. Candler took the bandage off and examined the small red cut with a scowling face. "How did this happen?" he asked curtly.

"One of Lopez's goons had a knife and liked to play games with helpless women," Micah said coldly.

"I hope he won't be doing it again," the physician murmured as he cleaned and redressed the superficial wound.

"That's classified," Micah said simply.

Callie glanced at him, surprised. His black eyes met hers, but he didn't say anything else.

"I'm going to give you a tetanus shot as a precaution," Dr. Candler said with a professional smile. "But I can almost guarantee that the cut won't leave a scar when it heals. I imagine it stings."

"A little," Callie agreed.

"I need to give her a full examination," Dr. Candler told him after giving Callie the shot. "Why don't you go outside and smoke one of those contraband Cuban cigars I'm not supposed to know you have?"

"They aren't contraband," Micah told him. "It isn't illegal if you get given one that someone has purchased in Cuba. Cobb was down there last month and he brought me back several."

"Leave it to you to find a legal way to do something illegal," Candler chuckled.

"Speaking of which, I'd better give a mutual acquaintance a quick call and thank him for the loan of his equipment." He glanced at Callie and smiled softly. "Then maybe Callie can relax while you finish here."

She didn't reply. He went out and closed the door behind him. She let out an audible sigh of relief.

"Now," Dr. Candler said as he continued to examine her. "Tell me what happened."

She did, still shaken and frightened by what she'd experienced in the last two days. He listened while he worked, his face giving nothing away.

"What happened to the man who did it?" he persisted.

She gave him an innocent smile. "I really don't know," she lied.

He sighed. "You and Micah." He shook his head. "Have you known him long?"

"Since I was fifteen," she told him. "His father and my mother were briefly married."

"You're Callie!" the doctor said at once.

# *Chapter Four*

The look on Callie's face was priceless. "How did you know?" she asked.

He smiled. "Micah talks about you a lot."

That was a shocker. "I didn't think he wanted anybody to know I even existed," she pointed out.

He pursed his lips. "Well, let's just say that he has ambiguous feelings about you."

Ambiguous. Right. Plainly stated, he couldn't stand her. But if that was true, why had he come himself to rescue her, instead of just sending his men?

She drew in a breath as he tended to her. "Am I going to be okay?"

"You're going to be good as new in a few days." He smiled at her. "Trust me."

"Micah seems to."

"He should. I taught him everything he knows

about surgery,'' he chuckled. ''I was a year ahead of him when we were in graduate school, and I took classes for one of the professors occasionally.''

She smiled. ''You're very good.''

''So was he,'' he replied grimly.

She hesitated, but curiosity prodded her on. ''If it wouldn't be breaking any solemn oath, could you tell me why he didn't finish his residency?''

He did, without going into details. ''He realized medicine wasn't his true calling.''

She nodded in understanding.

''But you didn't hear that from me,'' he added firmly.

''Oh, I never tell people things I know,'' she replied easily, smiling. ''I work for a lawyer.''

He chuckled. ''Do tell?''

''He's something of a fire-eater, but he's nice to me. He practices criminal law back in Jacobsville, Texas.''

He put the medical equipment to one side and told her she could get dressed.

''I'm going to put you on some antibiotics to fight off infection.'' He studied her with narrowed eyes. ''What you've been through is traumatic,'' he added as he handed her the prescription bottle. ''I'd advise counseling.''

''Right now,'' she said on a long breath, ''I'm occupied with just trying to stay alive. The drug dealer is still after me, you see.''

His jaw tautened. ''Micah will take care of you.''

''I know that.'' She stood up and smiled, extending her hand. ''Thanks.''

He shook her hand and shrugged. ''Think nothing

of it. We brilliant medical types feel obliged to minister to the masses…''

"Oh, for God's sake!" Micah groaned as he en-
tered the room, overhearing his friend.

Dr. Candler gave him a look full of frowning
mock-hauteur. "And aren't you lucky that I don't
have to examine *you* today?" he drawled.

"We're leaving. Right now." He took Callie by
the hand and gave the other man a grin. "Thanks."

"Anytime. You take care."

"You do the same."

Callie was herded out the door.

"But, the bill," she protested as he put her out a
side door and drew her into the vehicle that was waiting for them with the engine running.

"Already taken care of. Let's get to the airport."

Callie settled into the seat, still worrying. "I don't
have anything with me," she said miserably. "No
papers, no clothes, no shoes…"

"I told you, Maddie got all that together. It will
be waiting for us at the airport, along with tickets
and boarding passes."

"What if Lopez has people there waiting for us?"
she worried aloud.

"We also have people waiting there for us," Bojo
said from the front seat. "Miami is our safest do-
mestic port."

"Okay," she said, and smiled at him.

He smiled back.

Micah and Bojo exchanged a complicated glance.
Bojo turned his attention back to the road and didn't
say another word all the way to the airport. Callie
understood. Micah didn't want her getting too
friendly with his people. She didn't take offense. She

was used to rejection, after so many years in foster care. She only shrugged and looked out the window, watching palm trees and colorful buildings slide past as they wove through side streets and back onto the expressway.

The airport was crowded. Micah caught her by the arm and guided her past the ticket counter on the way to the concourses.

"But..." she protested.

"Don't argue. Just walk through the metal detector."

He followed close behind her. Neither of them was carrying anything metallic, but Micah was stopped when a security woman passed a wand over the two of them and her detector picked up the residual gunpowder on his hands and clothing. The woman looked at her instrument and then at him, with a wary, suspicious stare.

He smiled lazily at the uniformed woman holding the wand. "I'm on my way to a regional skeet shooting tournament," he lied glibly. "I sent my guns on ahead by express, unassembled. Can't be too careful these days, where firearms are concerned," he added, catching Callie's hand in his. "Right, honey?" he murmured softly, drawing her close.

To Callie's credit, she didn't faint at the unexpected feel of Micah's arm around her, but she tingled from head to toe and her heart went wild.

The airport security woman seemed to relax, and she smiled back. She assumed, as Micah had intended, that he and Callie were involved. "Indeed you can't. Have a good trip."

Micah kept that long, muscular arm around Callie

as they walked slowly down the concourse. He looked down, noting the erratic rhythm of her heartbeat at her neck, and he smiled to himself.

"You have lightning-quick reflexes," he remarked after a minute. "I noticed that in Cancún. You didn't argue, you didn't question anything I told you to do, and you moved almost as fast as I did. You're good company in tight corners."

She shrugged. "When you came in through the window, I didn't know who you were, because of that face mask. Actually," she confessed with a sheepish smile, "at first, I figured you were a rival drug dealer, but I had high hopes that you might be kind enough to just kill me and not torture me first if I didn't resist."

He drew in a sharp breath and the arm holding her contracted with a jerk. "Strange attitude, Callie," he remarked.

"Not at the time. Not to me, anyway." She shivered at the memory and felt his arm tighten almost protectively. They were well out of earshot and sight of the security guard. "Micah, what was that wand she was checking us with?"

"It detects nitrates," he replied. "With it, they can tell if a passenger has had any recent contact with weapons or explosives."

She was keenly aware of his arm still holding her close against his warm, powerful body. "You can, uh, let go now. She's out of sight."

He didn't relent. "Don't look, but there's a security guard with a two-way radio about fifteen feet to your right." He smiled down at her. "And I'll give you three guesses who's on the other end of it."

She smiled back, but it didn't reach her eyes. "The

lady with the nitrate wand? We're psyching them out, right?''

He searched her eyes and for a few seconds he stopped walking. "Psyching them out," he murmured. His gaze fell to her soft, full mouth. "Exactly."

She couldn't quite get her breath. His expression was unreadable, but his black eyes were glittering. He watched her blouse shake with the frantic rate of her heartbeats. He was remembering mistletoe and harsh words, and that same look in Callie's soft eyes, that aching need to be kissed that made her look so very vulnerable.

"What the hell," he murmured roughly as his head bent to hers. "It's an airport. People are saying hello and goodbye everywhere…"

His warm, hard mouth covered hers very gently while the sounds of people in transit all around them faded to a dull roar. His heavy brows drew together in something close to anguish as he began to kiss her. Fascinated by his expression, by the warm, ardent pressure of his mouth on hers, she closed her eyes tight, and fantasized that he meant it, that he wasn't pretending for the benefit of security guards, that he was enjoying the soft, tremulous response of her lips to the teasing, expert pressure of his own.

"Boss?"

They didn't hear the gruff whisper.

It was followed by the loud clearing of a throat and a cough.

They didn't hear that, either. Callie was on tiptoe now, her short nails digging into the hard muscles of his upper arms, hanging on Micah's slow, tender kiss with little more than willpower, so afraid that he was going to pull away...!

"Micah!" the voice said shortly.

Micah's head jerked up, and for a few seconds he seemed as disoriented as Callie. He stared blankly at the dark-headed man in front of him.

The man was extending a small case toward him. "Her papers and clothes and shoes and stuff," the man said, nodding toward Callie and clearing his throat again. "Maddie had me fly them over here."

"Thanks, Pogo."

The big, dark man nodded. He stared with open curiosity at Callie, and then he smiled gently. "It was my pleasure," he said, glancing again at Micah and making an odd little gesture with his head in Callie's direction.

"This is Callie Kirby," Micah said shortly, adding, "my...stepsister."

The big man's eyebrows levered up. "Oh! I mean, I was hoping she wasn't a real sister. I mean, the way you were kissing her and all." He flushed, and laughed self-consciously when Micah glared at him. Callie was scarlet, looking everywhere except at the newcomer.

"You'll miss your flight out of here," Micah said pointedly.

"What? Oh. Yeah." He grinned at Callie. "I'm Pogo. I'm from Saint Augustine. I used to wrestle alligators until Micah here gave me a job. I'm sort of a bodyguard, you know..."

"You're going to be an unemployed bodyguard in twenty seconds if you don't merge with the crowd," Micah said curtly.

"Oh. Well…sure. Bye, now," he told Callie with an ear-to-ear smile.

She smiled back. He was like a big teddy bear. She was sorry they wouldn't get to know each other.

Pogo almost fell over his own feet as he turned, jerking both busy eyebrows at his boss, before he melted into the crowd and vanished.

"Stop doing that," Micah said coldly.

She looked up at him blankly. "Doing what?"

"Smiling at my men like that. These men aren't used to it. Don't encourage them."

Her lips parted on a shaken breath. She looked at him as if she feared for his sanity. "Them?" she echoed, dazed.

"Bojo and Peter and Pogo," he said, moving restlessly. He was jealous. God knew why. It irritated him. "Come on."

He moved away from her, catching her hand tightly and pulling her along with him.

"And don't read anything into what just happened," he added coldly, without looking at her.

"Why would I?" she asked honestly. "You said it was just for appearances. I haven't forgotten how you feel about me, Micah."

He stopped and stared intently down into her eyes. His own were narrow, angry, impatient. She wore her heart where anyone could see it. Her vulnerability made him protective. Odd, that, when she was tough enough to survive captivity by Lopez and still keep her nerve during a bloody breakout.

"You don't have a clue how I feel about you," he said involuntarily. His fingers locked closer into hers. "I'm thirty-six. You're barely twenty-two. The sort of woman I prefer is sophisticated and street-smart and has no qualms about sex. You're still at the kissing-in-parked-cars stage.''

She flushed and searched his eyes. "I don't kiss people in parked cars because I don't date anybody," she told him with blunt honesty. "I can't leave Dad alone in the evenings. Besides, too many men around Jacobsville remember my mother, and think I'm like her." Her face stiffened and she looked away. "Including you."

He didn't speak. There was little softness left in him after all the violent years, but she was able to touch some last, sensitive place with her sweet voice. Waves of guilt ran over him. Yes, he'd compared her to her mother that Christmas. He'd said harsh, cruel things. He regretted them, but there was no going back. His feelings about Callie unnerved him. She was the only weak spot in his armor that he'd ever known. And what a good thing that she didn't know that, he told himself.

"You don't know what was really going on that night, Callie," he said after a minute.

She looked up at him. "Don't you think it's time I did?" she asked softly.

He toyed with her fingers, causing ripples of pleasure to run along her spine. "Why not? You're old enough to hear it now." He glanced around them cautiously before he looked at her again. "You were wearing an emerald velvet dress that night, the same one you'd worn to your eighteenth birthday party. They were watching a movie while you finished decorating the Christmas tree," he continued absently. "You'd just bent over to pick up an ornament when I came into the room. The dress had a deep neckline. You weren't wearing a bra under it, and your breasts were visible in that position, right to the nipples. You looked up at me and your nipples were suddenly hard.''

She gaped at him. The comment about her nipples was disturbing, but she had no idea what he meant by emphasizing them. ''I had no idea I was showing like that!''

''I didn't realize that. Not at first.'' He held her fingers tighter. ''You saw me and came right up against me, drowning me in that floral perfume you wore. You stood on tiptoe, like you did a minute ago, trying to tempt me into kissing you.''

She averted her embarrassed eyes. ''You said terrible things...''

''The sight of you like that had aroused me passionately,'' he said frankly, nodding when her shocked eyes jumped to his face. ''That's right. And I couldn't let you know it. I had to make you keep your distance, not an easy accomplishment after the alcohol you'd had. For which,'' he added coldly, ''your mother should have been shot! It was illegal for her to let you drink, even at home. Anyway, I read you the riot act, pushed you away and walked down the hall, right into your mother. She recognized immediately what you hadn't even noticed about my body, and she thought it was the sight of her in that slinky silver dress that had caused it. So she buried herself against me and started kissing me.'' He let out an angry breath. ''Your father saw us like that before I could push her away. And I couldn't tell him the truth, because you were just barely eighteen. I was already thirty-two.''

The bitterness in his deep voice was blatant. She didn't feel herself breathing. She'd only been eighteen, but he'd wanted her. She'd never realized it. Everything that didn't make sense was suddenly crystal clear—except that comment about his body. She wondered what her mother had seen and recognized about him that she hadn't.

"You never told me."

"You were a child, Callie," he said tautly. "In some ways, you still are. I was never low enough to take advantage of your innocence."

She was almost vibrating with the turmoil of her emotions. She didn't know what to do or say.

He drew in a long, slow breath as he studied her. "Come on," he said, tugging her along. "We have to move or we'll miss our flight." He handed her the case and indicated the ladies' room. "Get changed. I'll wait right here."

She nodded. Her mind was in such turmoil that she changed into jeans and a long-sleeved knit shirt, socks and sneakers, without paying much attention to what was in the small travel case. She didn't take time to look in any of the compartments, because he'd said to hurry. She glanced at herself in the mirror and was glad she had short hair that could do without a brush. Despite all she'd been through, it didn't look too bad. She'd have to buy a brush when they got where they were going, along with makeup and other toiletries. But that could wait.

Micah was propping up the wall when she came out. He nodded, approving what Maddie had packed for her, and took the case. "Here," he said, passing her a small plastic bag.

Inside were makeup, a brush, a toothbrush, toothpaste and deodorant. She almost cried at the thoughtful gift.

"Thanks," she said huskily.

Micah pulled the tickets and boarding passes out of his shirt pocket. "Get out your driver's license and birth certificate," he said. "We have to have a photo ID to board."

She felt momentary panic. "My birth certificate is in my file at home, and my driver's license is still in my purse, in my car...!"

He laid a lean forefinger across her pretty mouth, slightly swollen from the hard contact with his. "Your car is at your house, and your purse is inside it, and it's locked up tight. I told Maddie to put your birth certificate and your driver's license in the case. Have you looked for them?"

"No. I didn't think..."

She paused, putting the case down on the carpeted concourse floor to open it. Sure enough, her driver's license was in the zipped compartment that she hadn't looked in when she was in the bathroom. Besides that, the unknown Maddie had actually put her makeup and toiletries inside as well, in a plastic bag. She could have wept at the woman's thoughtfulness, but she wasn't going to tell Micah and make him feel uncomfortable that he'd already bought her those items. She closed it quickly and stuck her license in her jeans pocket.

"Does Maddie really look like me?" she asked on the way to the ticket counter, trying not to sound as if she minded. He'd said they resembled one another earlier.

"At a distance," he affirmed. "Her hair is shorter than yours, and she's more muscular. She was a karate instructor when she signed on with me. She's twenty-six."

"Karate."

"Black belt," he added.

"She seems to be very efficient," she murmured a little stiffly.

He gave her a knowing glance that she didn't see and chuckled softly. "She's in love with Colby Lane, a guy I used to work with at the justice department," he told her. "She signed on with us because she thought he was going to."

"He didn't?"

He shook his head. "He's working for Pierce Hutton's outfit, as a security chief, along with Tate Winthrop, an acquaintance of mine."

"Oh."

They were at the ticket counter now. He held out his hand for her driver's license and birth certificate, and presented them along with his driver's license and passport and the tickets to the agent on duty.

She put the tickets in a neat folder with the boarding passes in a slot on the outside, checked the ID, and handed them back.

"Have a nice trip," she told them. "We'll be boarding in just a minute."

Callie hadn't looked at her boarding pass. She was too busy trying to spot Bojo and Peter and the others.

"They're already en route," Micah told her nonchalantly, having guessed why she was looking around her.

"They aren't going with us?"

He gave her a wry glance. "Somebody had to bring my boat back. I left it here in the marina when I flew out to Jacobsville to help Eb Scott and Cy Parks shut down Lopez's drug operation. It's still there."

"Why couldn't we have gone on the boat, too?"

"You get seasick," he said before he thought.

Her lips fell open. She'd only been on a boat once, with him and her mother and stepfather, when she was sixteen. They'd gone to San Antonio and sailed down the river on a tour boat. She'd gotten very sick and thrown up. It had been Micah who'd looked after her, to his father's amusement.

She hadn't even remembered the episode until he'd said that. She didn't get seasick now, but she kept quiet.

"Besides," he added, avoiding her persistent stare, "if Lopez does try anything, it won't be on an international flight out of the U.S. He's in enough trouble with the higher-ups in his organization without making an assault on a commercial plane just to get even for losing a prisoner."

She relaxed a little, because that had been on her mind.

He took her arm and drew her toward a small door, where a uniformed man was holding a microphone. He announced that they were boarding first-class passengers first, and Micah ushered her right down the ramp and into the plane.

"First class," she said, dazed, as he eased her into a wide, comfortable seat with plenty of leg room. Even for a man of his height, there was enough of it.

"Always," he murmured, amused at her fascination. "I don't like cramped places."

She fastened her seat belt with a wry smile. "Considering the size of you, I can understand that. Micah, what about Dad?" she added, ashamed that she was still belaboring the point.

''Maddie's got him under surveillance. When Pogo goes back, he'll work a split shift with her at your apartment to safeguard him. Eb and Cy are keeping their eyes out, as well. I promise you, Dad's going to be safe.'' He hesitated, searching her wide, pale blue eyes. ''But you're the one in danger.''

''Because I got away,'' she agreed, nodding.

He seemed worried. His dark eyes narrowed on her face. ''Lopez doesn't lose prisoners, ever. You're the first. Someone is going to pay for that. He'll make an example of the people who didn't watch you closely enough. Then he'll make an example of you and me, if he can, to make sure his reputation doesn't suffer.''

She shivered involuntarily. It was a nightmare that would haunt her forever. She remembered what she'd suffered already and her eyes closed on a helpless wave of real terror.

''You're going to be safe, Callie. Listen,'' he said, reading her expression, ''I live on a small island in the Bahamas chain, not too far from New Providence. I have state-of-the-art surveillance equipment and a small force of mercenaries that even Lopez would hesitate to confront. Lopez isn't the only one who has a reputation in terrorist circles. Before I put together my team and hired out as a professional soldier, I worked for the CIA.''

Her eyes widened. She hadn't known that. She hadn't known anything about him.

''They approached me while I was in college, before I changed my course of study to medicine. I was already fluent in French and Dutch, and I picked up German in my sophomore year. I couldn't blend in very well in an Arabic country, but I could pass for

German or Dutch, and I did. During holidays and vacations, I did a lot of traveling for the company.'' He smiled, reminiscing. ''It was dangerous work, and exciting. By the time I was in my last year of residency, I knew for a fact that I wouldn't be able to settle down into a medical practice. I couldn't live without the danger. That's when I left school for good.''

She was hanging on every word. It was amazing to have him speak to her as an equal, as an adult. They'd never really talked before.

''I wondered,'' she said, ''why you gave it up.''

He stretched his long legs out in front of him and crossed his arms over his broad chest. ''I had the skills, but as I grew older, the less I wanted roots or anything that hinted at permanence. I don't want marriage or children, so a steady, secure profession seemed superfluous. On the other hand, being a mercenary is right up my alley. I live for those surges of adrenaline.''

''None of us ever knew about that,'' she said absently, trying not to let him see how much it hurt to know that he couldn't see a future as a husband and father. Now that she knew what he really did for a living, she could understand why. He was never going to be a family man. ''We thought it was the trust your mother left you that kept you in Armani suits,'' she added in a subdued tone.

''No, it wasn't. I like my lifestyle,'' he added with a pointed glance in her direction. He stretched lazily, pulling the silk shirt he was wearing taut across the muscles of his chest. A flight attendant actually hesitated as she started down the aisle, helplessly drinking in the sight of him. He was a dish, all right. Callie didn't blame the other woman for staring, but the flight attendant had blond hair and blue eyes and she was lovely. Her beauty was like a knife in the ribs to Callie, pointing out all the physical attributes she herself lacked. If only she'd been pretty, she told herself miserably, maybe Micah would have wanted more than an occasional kiss from her.

"Would you care for anything to drink, sir?" the flight attendant asked, smiling joyfully as she paused by Micah's side.

"Scotch and soda," he told her. He smiled ruefully. "It's been a long day."

"Coming right up," the woman said, and went at once to get the order.

Callie noticed that she hadn't been asked if she wanted anything. She wondered what Micah would say if she asked for a neat whiskey. Probably nothing, she told herself miserably. He might have kissed her in the airport, but he only seemed irritated by her now.

The flight attendant was back with his drink. She glanced belatedly at Callie and grimaced. "Sorry," she told the other woman. "I didn't think to ask if you'd like something, too?"

Callie shook her head and smiled. "No, I don't want anything, thanks."

"Are you stopping in Nassau or just passing through?" the woman asked Micah boldly.

He gave her a lingering appraisal, from her long, elegant legs to her full breasts and lovely face. He smiled. "I live there."

"Really!" Her eyes lit as if they'd concealed fires. "So do I!"

"Then you must know Lisette Dubonnet," he said.

"Dubonnet," the uniformed woman repeated, frowning. "Isn't her father Jacques Dubonnet, the French ambassador?"

"Yes," he said. "Lisette and I have known each other for several years. We're…very good friends."

The flight attendant looked suddenly uncomfortable, and a little flushed. Micah was telling her, in a nice way, that she'd overstepped her introduction. He smiled to soften the rejection, but it was a rejection, just the same.

"Miss Dubonnet is very lovely," the flight attendant said with a pleasant, if more formal, smile. "If you need anything else, just ring."

"I will."

She went on down the aisle. Beside him, Callie was staring out the window at the ocean below without any real enthusiasm. She hated her own reaction to the news that Micah was involved with some beautiful woman in Nassau. And not only a beautiful woman, but a poised sophisticate as well.

"You'll like Lisse," he said carelessly. "I'll ask her to go shopping with you. You'll have to have a few clothes. She has excellent taste."

Implying that Callie had none at all. Her heart felt like iron in her chest, heavy and cold. "That would be nice," she said, lying through her teeth. "I won't need much, though," she added, thinking about her small savings account.

"You may be there longer than a day or two," he said in a carefully neutral voice. "You can't wear the same clothes day in and day out. Besides,'' he added curtly, ''it's about time you learned how to dress like a young woman instead of an elderly recluse!''

## Chapter Five

Callie felt the anger boil out of her in waves. "Oh, that's nice, coming from you," she said icily. "When you're the one who started me wearing that sort of thing in the first place!"

"Me?" he replied, his eyebrows arching.

"You said I dressed like a tramp," she began, and her eyes were anguished as she remembered the harsh, hateful words. "Like my mother," she added huskily. "You said that I flaunted my body..." She stopped suddenly and wrapped her arms around herself. She stared out the porthole while she recovered her self-control. "Sorry," she said stiffly. "I've been through a lot. It's catching up with me. I didn't mean to say that."

He felt as if he'd been slapped. Maybe he deserved it, too. Callie had been beautiful in that green velvet dress. The sight of her in it had made him ache. She had the grace and poise of a model, even if she lacked the necessary height. But he'd never realized that his own anger had made her ashamed of her body, and at such an impressionable age. Good God, no wonder she dressed like a dowager! Then he remembered what she'd hinted in the jungle about the foster homes she'd stayed in, and he wondered with real anguish what she'd endured before she came to live in his father's house. There had to be more to her repression than just a few regretted words from him.

"Callie," he said huskily, catching her soft chin and turning her flushed face toward him. "Something happened to you at one of those foster homes, didn't it?"

She bit her lower lip and for a few seconds, there was torment in her eyes.

He drew in a sharp breath.

She turned her face away again, embarrassed.

"Can you talk about it?" he asked.

She shook her head jerkily.

His dark eyes narrowed. And her mother—her own mother—had deserted her, had placed her in danger with pure indifference. "Damn your mother," he said in a gruff whisper.

She didn't look at him again. At least, she thought mistakenly, he was remembering the breakup of his father's marriage, and not her childhood anymore. She didn't like remembering the past.

He leaned back in his seat and stretched, folding his arms over his broad chest. One day, he promised himself, there was going to be a reckoning for Callie's mother. He hoped the woman got just a fraction of what she deserved, for all the grief and pain she'd caused. Although, he had to admit, she had changed in the past year or so.

He wondered if her mother's first husband, Kane Kirby, had contacted Callie recently. Poor kid, he thought. She really had gone through a lot, even before Lopez had her kidnapped. He thought about what she'd suffered at Lopez's hands, and he ached to avenge her. The drug lord was almost certain to make a grab for her again. But this time, he promised himself, Lopez was going to pay up his account in full. He owed Callie that much for the damage he'd done.

It was dark when the plane landed in Nassau at the international airport, and Micah let Callie go ahead of him down the ramp to the pavement. The moist heat was almost smothering, after the air-conditioned plane. Micah took her arm and escorted her to passport control. He glanced with amusement at the passengers waiting around baggage claim for their bags to be unloaded. Even when he traveled routinely, he never took more than a duffel bag that he could carry into the airplane with him. It saved time waiting for luggage to be off-loaded.

After they checked through, he moved her outside again and hailed a cab to take them to the marina, where the boat was waiting.

Another small round of formalities and they boarded the sleek, powerful boat that already contained Micah's men. Callie went below and sat quietly on a comfortable built-in sofa, watching out the porthole as the boat flew out of Prince George Wharf and around the bay. From there, it went out to sea.

"Comfortable?" Micah asked, joining her below.

She nodded. "It's so beautiful out there. I love the way the ships light up at night. I knew cruise ships did, but I didn't realize that smaller ones did, too." She glanced at him in the subdued light of the cabin. "You don't light yours, do you?"

He chuckled. "In my line of work, it wouldn't be too smart, would it?"

"Sorry," she said with a sheepish smile. "I wasn't thinking."

He poured himself a scotch and water and added ice cubes. "Want something to drink? If you don't want anything alcoholic, I've got soft drinks or fruit juice."

She shook her head. "I'm fine." She laughed. Her eyes caught and held on a vessel near the lighted dock. "Look! There's a white ship with black sails flying a skull and crossbones Jolly Roger flag!"

He chuckled. "That would be Fred Spence. He's something of a local eccentric. Nice boat, though."

She glanced at him. "This one is nice, too."

"It's comfortable on long hauls," he said noncommittally. He dropped down onto the sofa beside her and crossed his long legs. "We need to talk."

"About what?"

"Lopez. I'm putting you under twenty-four-hour surveillance," he said somberly. "If I'm not within yelling distance, one of my men will be. Even when you go shopping with Lisse, Bojo or Peter will go along. You aren't to walk on the beach alone, ever."

"But surely that would be safe...?"

He sat forward abruptly, and his black eyes glittered. "Callie, he has weapons that could pinpoint your body heat and send a missile after it from a distance of half a mile," he said curtly.

She actually gasped. That brought to mind another worry. She frowned. "I'm putting you in jeopardy by being with you," she said suddenly.

"You've got that backward, honey," he said, the endearment coming so naturally that he wasn't even aware he'd used it until he watched Callie's soft complexion flush. "You were in jeopardy in the first place because of me. Why does it make you blush when I call you honey?" he added immediately, the question quick enough to rattle her.

"I'm not used to it."

"From me," he drawled softly. "Or from any man?"

She shifted. "From Dad, maybe."

"Dad doesn't count. I mean single, datable bachelors."

She shook her head. "I don't date."

He'd never connected her solitary existence with himself. Now, he was forced to. He drew his breath in sharply, and got up from the sofa. He took a long sip from his drink, walking slowly over to stare out the porthole at the distant lights of the marina as they left it behind. "I honestly didn't realize how much damage I did to your ego, Callie. I'm really sorry about it."

"I was just as much at fault as you were," she replied evenly. "I shouldn't have thrown myself at you like some drunk prostitute..."

"Callie!" he exclaimed, horrified at her wording.

She averted her eyes and her hands clenched in her lap. "Well, I did."

He put his drink on the bar and knelt just in front of her. He was so tall that his black eyes were even with soft blue ones in the position. His lean hands went to her waist and he shook her very gently.

"I pushed you away because I wanted you, not because I thought you were throwing yourself at me," he said bluntly. "I was afraid that I wouldn't be able to resist you if I didn't do something very fast. I would have explained it to you eventually, if your mother hadn't stepped in and split the family apart, damn her cold heart!"

Her hands rested hesitantly on his broad shoulders, lifted and then rested again while she waited to see if she was allowed to touch him.

He seemed to realize that, because he smiled very slowly and his thumbs edged out against her flat belly in a sensuous stroking motion. "I like being touched," he murmured. "It's all right."

She smiled nervously. "I'm not used to doing it."

"I noticed." He stood up and drew her up with him. The top of her head only came to his nose. He framed her face in his warm, strong hands and lifted it gently. "Want to kiss me?" he asked in a husky whisper, and his eyes fell to her own soft mouth.

She wasn't sure about that. Her hands were on his chest now, touching lightly over the silky fabric. Under it, she could feel thick hair. She was hopelessly curious about what he looked like bare-chested. She'd never seen Micah without a shirt in all the time she'd lived in his house with his father.

"No pressure," he promised, bending. "And I won't make fun of you."

"Make fun of me?" she asked curiously.

"Never mind." He bent and his lips closed tenderly on her upper lip while he tasted the moist inside of it with his tongue. His lips moved to her lower lip and repeated the arousing little caress. His hands were at her waist, but they began to move up and down with a lazy, sensual pressure that made her body go rigid in his arms.

He lifted his mouth from her face and looked down at her with affectionate amusement. "Relax! Why are you afraid of me?" he asked gently. "I wouldn't hurt you, Callie. Not for any reason."

"I know. It's just that…"

"What?" he asked.

Her eyes met his plaintively. "Don't…tease me," she asked with dignity. "I'm not experienced enough to play that sort of game."

The amusement left his face. "Is that what it seems like to you?" he asked. He searched her worried eyes. "Even if I were into game-playing, you'd never be a target. I do have some idea now of what you've been through, in the past and just recently."

She let out the breath she'd been holding. "This Lisette you mentioned. Is she…important to you?"

"We're good friends," he said, and there was a new remoteness in his expression. "You'll like her. She's outgoing and she loves people. She'll help you get outfitted."

Now she was really worried. "I have my credit card, but I can't afford expensive shops," she emphasized. "Could you tell her that, so I won't have to?"

"I can tell her." He smiled quizzically. "But why won't you let me buy you some clothes?"

"I'm not your responsibility, even if you have been landed with me, Micah," she replied. "I pay my own way."

He wondered if she had any idea how few of his

female acquaintances would ever have made such a statement to him? It occurred to him that he'd never had a woman refuse a wardrobe.

He scowled. "You could pay me back, if you have to."

She smiled. "Thanks. But I'll buy my own clothes."

His black eyes narrowed on her face. "You were always independent," he recalled.

"I've had to be. I've been basically on my own for a long time," she said matter-of-factly. "Since I was a kid, really, and my father—I mean, Mother's first husband—threw us out. Mother didn't want the responsibility for me by herself and Kane Kirby didn't want me at all."

"If your father didn't think you were his, why didn't he have a DNA profile run?" he asked with a watchful look.

She drew away from him. "There was no such thing fifteen years ago."

"You could insist that he have it done now, couldn't you?" He gave her an odd look. "Have you spoken to him?"

"He phoned me recently. But I didn't call him back," she said unwillingly. She'd seen her mother's first husband once or twice, during his rare visits to his Jacobsville home. He'd actually phoned her apartment a few weeks ago and left a strange, tentative message asking her to call him back. She never had. His rejection of her still hurt. She didn't see him often. He lived mostly in Miami these days.

"Why not talk to him and suggest the DNA test?" he persisted.

She looked up at him with tired, sad eyes. "Because it would probably prove what my mother said, that I'm not related to him at all.'' She smiled faintly. ''I don't know whose child I am. And it really doesn't matter anymore. Please, just...leave it alone.''

He sighed with irritation, as if he knew more than he was telling her. She wondered why he was so interested in her relationship with the man who was supposed to be her own father.

He saw that curiosity in her eyes, and he closed up. He could see years of torment in that sad little face. It infuriated him. ''Your mother should be horsewhipped for what she did to you,'' he said flatly.

She folded her arms across her chest, remembering the loneliness of her young life reluctantly. New homes, new faces, new terrors. She turned back to the porthole. ''I used to wish I had someplace to belong,'' she confessed. ''I was always the outsider, in any home where I lived. Until my mother married your father,'' she added, smiling. ''I thought he'd be like all the others, that he'd either ignore me or be too familiar, but he just sort of belonged to me, from the very beginning. He really cared about me. He hugged me, coming and going.'' She drew in a soft breath. ''You can't imagine what it feels like, to have someone hug you, when you've hardly been touched in your whole life except in bad ways. He was forever teasing me, bringing me presents. He became my family. He even made up for my mother. I couldn't help loving him.'' She turned, surprised to see an odd look of self-contempt on Micah's strong face. ''I guess you resented us...''

''I resented your mother, Callie,'' he interrupted,

feeling icy-cold inside. "What I felt for you was a lot more complicated than that."

She gave him a surprised little smile. "But, I'm still my mother's daughter, right? Don't they say, look at the mother and you'll see the daughter in twenty years or so?"

His face hardened. "You'll never be like her. Not in your worst nightmares."

She sighed. "I wish I could be sure of that."

He felt like hitting something. "Do you know where she is?"

"Somewhere in Europe with her new husband, I suppose," she said indifferently. "Dad's lawyer heard from her year before last. She wanted a copy of the final divorce decree, because she was getting married again, to some British nobleman, the lawyer said."

He remembered his own mother, a gentle little brown-eyed woman with a ready smile and open arms. She'd died when he was ten, and from that day on, he and his father had been best friends. Until Anna showed up, with her introverted, nervous teenage daughter. The difference between Anna and his own mother was incredible. Anna was selfish, vain, greedy…he could have laid all seven deadly sins at her feet with ease. But Callie was nothing like her, except, perhaps, her exact opposite.

"You're the sort of woman who would love a big family," he murmured thoughtfully.

She laughed. "What do I know about families?" she responded. "I'd be terrified of bringing an innocent child into this sort of world, knowing what I know about the uncertainties of life."

He shoved his hands into his pockets. Children.

He'd never thought about them. But he could picture Callie with a baby in her arms, and it seemed perfectly natural. She'd had some bad breaks, but she'd love her own child. It was sad that she didn't want kids.

"Anyway, marriage is dead last on my list of things to do," she added, uncomfortable because he wasn't saying anything.

"That makes two of us," he murmured. It was the sort of thing he always said, but it didn't feel as comfortable suddenly as it used to. He wondered why.

She turned away from the porthole. "How long will it take us to get to your place?" she asked.

He shrugged. "About twenty more minutes, at this speed," he said, smiling. "I think you'll like it. It's old, and rambling, and it has a history. According to the legend, a local pirate owned it back in the eighteenth century. He kidnapped a highborn Spanish lady and married her out of hand. They had six children together and lived a long and happy life, or so the legend goes." He studied her curiously. "Isn't there Spanish in your ancestry somewhere?"

Her face closed up. "Don't ask me. My mother always said she descended from what they call 'black Irish,' from when the Spanish armada was shipwrecked off the coast of Ireland. I know her hair was jet-black when she was younger, and she has an olive complexion. But I don't really know her well enough to say whether or not it was the truth."

He bit off a comment on her mother's penchant for lying. "Your complexion isn't olive," he remarked quietly. "It's creamy. Soft."

He embarrassed her. She averted her eyes. "I'm just ordinary."

He shook his head. His eyes narrowed on her pretty bow of a mouth. "You always were unique, Callie." He hesitated. "Callie. What's it short for?" he asked, suddenly curious.

She drew in a slow breath. "Colleen," she replied reluctantly. "But nobody ever calls me that. It's been Callie since I was old enough to talk."

"Colleen what?"

"Colleen Mary," she replied.

He smiled. "Yes. That suits you."

He was acting very strangely. In fact, he had been ever since he rescued her. She wondered if he was still trying to take her mind off Lopez. If he was, it wasn't working. The nightmarish memories were too fresh to forget.

She looked at him worriedly. "Lopez will be looking for me," she said suddenly.

He tautened. "Let him look," he said shortly. "If he comes close enough to make a target, I'll solve all his problems. He isn't getting his hands on you again, Callie."

She relaxed a little. He sounded very confident. It made her feel better. She moved back into the center of the room, wrapping her arms around herself. "How can people like that exist in a civilized world?" she wanted to know.

"Because governments still can't fight that kind of wealth," he said bluntly. "Money and power make criminals too formidable. But we've got the Rico statutes which help us take away some of that illegal money," he added, "and we've got dedicated people enforcing the law. We win more than we lose these days.''

''You sound like a government agent,'' she teased.

He chuckled. ''I do, don't I? I spent several years being one. It sticks.'' He moved forward, taking his hands out of his pockets to wrap them gently around her upper arms. ''I give you my word that I won't let Lopez get you. In case you were worrying about that.''

She grimaced. ''Does it show?''

''I don't know. Maybe I can read your mind these days,'' he added, trying to make light of it.

''You're sure? About Dad being safe, I mean?''

''I'm sure about Dad,'' he returned at once. ''Gator may look dumb, but he's got a mind like a steel trap, and he's quick on the draw. Nobody's going to get past him—certainly nobody's going to get past him and Maddie at the same time.''

''You like her a lot, I guess?''

He chuckled. ''Yes, I do. She's hell on two legs, and one of the best scroungers I've ever had.''

''What does Bojo do?''

He gave her a wary appraisal, and it seemed as if he didn't like the question. ''Bojo is a small arms expert,'' he replied. ''He also has relatives in most of the Muslim nations, so he's a great source of information as well. Peter, you met him on the plane, is new with the group. He's a linguist and he's able to pass for an Arab or an Israeli. He's usually undercover in any foreign operation we're hired to undertake. You haven't met Rodrigo yet—he was the pilot of the DC-3 we flew back to Miami. He does undercover work as well. Don, the blond copilot, is a small arms expert. We have another operative,

Cord Romero, who does demolition work for us, but he had an accident and he's out of commission for a while.''

"What you and your men do—it's dangerous work."

"Living is dangerous work," he said flatly. "I like the job. I don't have any plans to give it up."

Her eyebrows arched and her pale blue eyes twinkled. "My goodness, did I propose marriage just now and get instant amnesia afterward? Excuse *me!*"

He gaped at her. "Propose marriage...?"

She held up both hands. "Now, don't get ruffled. I understand how men feel about these things. I haven't asked you out, or sent you flowers, or even bought you a nice pair of earrings. Naturally you're miffed because I put the cart before the horse and asked you to give up an exciting job you love for marriage to a boring paralegal."

He blinked. "Callie?" he murmured, obviously fearing for her sanity.

"We'll just forget the proposal," she offered generously.

"You didn't propose!" he gritted.

"See? You've already forgotten. Isn't that just like a man?" she muttered, as she went back to the sofa and sat down. "Now you'll pout for an hour because I rejected you."

He burst out laughing when he realized what she was doing. It took the tension away from their earlier discussion and brought them back to normal. He dropped down into an armchair across from her and folded his arms over his chest.

"Just when I think I've got you figured out, you throw me another curve," he said appreciatively.

"Believe me, if I didn't have a sense of humor, I'd already have smeared Mr. Kemp with honey and locked him in a closet with a grizzly bear."

"Ouch!"

"I thought you lived in Nassau?" She changed the subject.

He shrugged. "I did. This place came on the market three years ago and I bought it. I like the idea of having a defendable property. You'll see what I mean when we get there. It's like a walled city."

"I'll bet there are lots of flowers," she murmured hopefully.

"Millions," he confirmed. "Hibiscus and orchids and bougainvillea. You'll love it." He smiled gently. "You were always planting things when I lived at home."

"I didn't think you noticed anything I did," she replied before she thought.

He watched her quietly. "Your mother spent most of that time ordering you around," he recalled. "If she wanted a soft drink, or a scarf, or a sandwich, she always sent you after it. I don't recall that she ever touched a vacuum cleaner or a frying pan the whole time she was around."

"I learned to cook in the last foster home I stayed in," she said with a smile. "It was the best of the lot. Mrs. Toms liked me. She had five little kids and she had arthritis real bad. She was so sweet that it was a joy to help her. She was always surprised that anyone would want to do things for her."

"Most giving people are," he replied. "Ironically they're usually the last ones people give to."

"That's true."

"What else did she teach you?" he asked.

"How to crochet," she recalled. She sighed. "I can't make sweaters and stuff, but I taught myself how to make hats. I give them to children and old people in our neighborhood. I work on them when I'm waiting for appointments with Dad. I get through a lot."

It was another reminder that she was taking care of his father, something he should have been doing himself—something he would be doing, if Callie's mother hadn't made it impossible for him to be near his parent.

"You're still bitter about Dad," she said, surprising him. "I can tell. You get this terrible haunted look in your eyes when I talk about him."

It surprised him that at her age she could read him so well, when his own men couldn't. He wasn't sure he liked it.

"I miss him," he confessed gruffly. "I'm sorry he won't let me make peace."

She gaped at him. "Whoever told you that?"

He hesitated. "I haven't tried to talk to him in years. So I phoned him a few days ago, before you were kidnapped. He listened for a minute and hung up without saying a word."

"What day was it?"

"It was Saturday. What difference does that make?"

"What time was it?" she repeated.

"Noon."

She smiled gently. "I go to get groceries at noon on Saturdays, because Mrs. Ruiz, who lives next door, comes home for lunch and makes it for herself and Dad and stays with him while I'm away."

"So?"

"So, Mrs. Ruiz doesn't speak English yet, she's still learning. The telephone inhibits her. She'll answer it, but if it's not me, she'll put it right down again." She smiled. "That's why I asked when you called."

"Then, Dad might talk to me, if I tried again," he said after a minute.

"Micah, he loves you," she said softly. "You're the only child he has. Of course he'll talk to you. He doesn't know what really happened with my mother, no more than I did, until you told me the truth. But he realizes now that if it hadn't been you, it would have been some other younger man. He said that, after the divorce was final, she even told him so."

"He didn't try to get in touch with me."

"He was upset for a long time after it happened. So was I. We blamed you both. But that's in the past. He'd love to hear from you now," she assured him. "He didn't think you'd want to talk to him, after so much time had passed and after what he'd said to you. He feels bad about that."

He leaned forward. "If that's so, when he had the heart attack, why wasn't I told?"

"I called the only number I had for you," she said. "I never got an answer. The hospital said they'd try to track you down, but I guess they didn't."

Could it really be that simple? he wondered. "That was at the old house, in Nassau. It was disconnected three years ago. The number I have now is unlisted."

"Oh."

"Why didn't you ask Eb Scott or Cy Parks?"

"I don't know them," she said hesitantly. "And until very recently, when this Lopez thing made the

headlines, I didn't know they were mercenaries.''
She averted her eyes. ''I knew you were acquainted
with them, but I certainly didn't know that you were
one of them.''

He took a slow breath. No, he remembered, she
didn't know. He'd never shared that bit of information with either her or Jack Steele.

''I wrote to you, too, about the heart attack, at the
last address you left us.''

''That would have been forwarded. I never got it.''

''I sent it,'' she said.

''I'm not doubting that you did. I'm telling you
that it never got to me.''

''I'm really sorry,'' she told him. ''I did try, even
if it doesn't look like it. I always hoped that you'd
eventually phone someone and I'd be able to contact
you. When you didn't, well, I guess Dad and I both
figured that you weren't interested in what happened
back here. And he did say that he'd been very cruel
in what he said to you when you left.''

''He was. But I understood,'' he added.

She smiled sadly. ''He loves you. When this is
over, you should make peace with him. I think you'll
find that he'll more than meet you halfway. He's
missed you terribly.''

''I've missed him, too.'' He could have added that
he'd missed her as well, but she wasn't likely to believe him.

He started to speak, but he felt the boat slowing.
He smiled. ''We must be coming up to the pier.
Come on. It will be nice to have a comfortable bed
to sleep in tonight.''

She nodded, and followed him up to the deck.

Her eyes caught sight of the house, on a small rise
in the distance, long and low and lighted. She could

see arches and flowers, even in the darkness, because of the solar-powered lights that lined the walkway from the pier up to the walled estate. She caught her breath. It was like a house she'd once seen in a magazine and daydreamed about as a child. She had the oddest feeling that she was coming home...

## Chapter Six

"What do you think?" Micah asked as he helped her onto the ramp that led down to the pier.

"It's beautiful," she said honestly. "I expect it's even more impressive in the daylight."

"It is." He hesitated, turning back toward the men who still on the boat. "Bojo! Make sure we've got at least two guards on the boat before you come up to the house," he called to his associate, who grinned and replied that he would. "Peter can help you," he added involuntarily.

Callie didn't seem to notice that he'd jettisoned both men who'd been friendly with her. Micah did. He didn't like the idea of his men getting close to her. It wasn't jealousy. Of course it wasn't. He was...protecting her from complications.

She looked around as they went up the wide graveled path to the house, frowning as she became aware of odd noises. "What's that sound?" she asked Micah.

He smiled lazily. "My early warning radar."

"Huh?"

He chuckled. "I keep a flock of geese," he explained, nodding toward a fenced area where a group of big white birds walked around and swam in a huge pool of water. "Believe it or not, they're better than guard dogs."

"Wouldn't a guard dog or two be a better idea?"

"Nope. I've got a Mac inside."

Before she could ask any more questions, the solid wood front door opened and a tall, imposing man in khakis with gray-sprinkled black wavy hair stood in their path. He was holding an automatic weapon in one big hand.

"Welcome home, boss," he said in deep, crisply accented British. He grinned briefly and raised two bushy eyebrows at the sight of Callie. "Got her, did you?"

"Got her, and with no casualties," Micah replied, returning the grin. "How's it going, Mac?"

"No worries. But it'll rain soon." He shifted his weight, grimacing a little.

"At least you're wearing the prosthesis, now," Micah muttered as he herded Callie into the house.

Mac rubbed his hip after he closed the door and followed them. "Damned thing feels funny," he said. "And I can't run." He glowered at Micah as if the whole thing was his fault.

"Hey," Micah told him, "didn't I say 'duck'? In fact, didn't I say it twice?"

"You said it, but I had my earphones in!"

"Excuses, excuses. We even took up a collection

for your funeral, then you had to go mess everything up by living!'' Micah grumbled.

"Oh, sure, after you lot had divided up all my possessions! Bojo's still got my favorite shirt and he won't give it back! And he doesn't even wear shirts!''

"He's using it to polish his gun,'' Micah explained. "Says it's the best shine he's ever put on it.''

Callie was openly gaping at them.

Micah's black eyes twinkled. "We're joking,'' he told her gently. "It's the way we let off steam, so that we don't get bogged down in worry. What we do is hard work, and dangerous. We have to have safety valves.''

"I'll blow Bojo's safety valve for him if he doesn't give back my shirt!'' Mac assured his boss. "And you haven't even introduced us.''

Callie smiled and held out her hand. "Hi! I'm Callie Kirby.''

"I'm MacPherson,'' he replied, shaking it. "I took a mortar hit on our last mission, so I've got KP until I get used to this damned prosthesis,'' he added, lifting his right leg and grimacing.

"You'd better get used to it pretty soon, or you're going to be permanent in that kitchen,'' Micah assured him. "Now I'd like to get Callie settled. She's been through a lot.''

The other man became somber all at once. "She's not what I expected,'' Mac said reluctantly as he studied her.

"I can imagine,'' she said with a sad little smile. "You were expecting a woman who was blond and as good-looking as Micah. I know I don't look like him..."

Before she could add that they weren't related, the older man interrupted her. "That isn't what I meant," Mac replied at once.

She shrugged and smiled carelessly. "Of course not. I really am tired," she added.

"Come on," Micah said. "Have you got something for sandwiches?" Micah asked Mac. "We didn't stop for food."

"Sure," Mac replied, visibly uncomfortable. "I'll get right to it."

Micah led Callie down the long hall and turned her into a large, airy room with a picture window overlooking the ocean. Except for the iron bars, it looked very touristy.

"Mac does most of the cooking. We used to take turns, but after he was wounded, and we found out that his father once owned a French restaurant, we gave him permanent KP." He glanced at her with a wry smile. "We thought it might encourage him to put on the prosthesis and try to be rehabilitated. Apparently it's working."

"He's very nice."

He closed the door and turned to her, his face somber. "He meant that the sort of woman I usually bring here is blond and long-legged and buxom, and that they usually ignore the hired help."

She flushed. "You didn't have to explain."

"Didn't I?" His eyes narrowed on her face as a potential complication presented itself when he thought about having Lisette take Callie on that shopping trip. The woman was extremely jealous, and Callie had been through enough turmoil already.

"I haven't told Mac or Lisette that we aren't related. It might be as well to let them continue thinking we are, for the time being."

She wondered why, but she wasn't going to lower her pride by asking. "Sure," she said with careful indifference. "No problem." Presumably this Lisette would be jealous of a stepsister, but not of a real one. Micah obviously didn't want to cause waves. She smiled drowsily. "I think I could sleep the clock around."

"If Maddie's her usual efficient self, she should have packed a nightgown for you."

"I don't have a gown," she murmured absently, glancing at the case he'd put down beside the bed.

"Pajamas, then."

"Uh, I don't wear those, either."

He stood up and looked at her pointedly. "What *do* you sleep in?"

She cleared her throat. "Never mind."

His eyebrows arched. "Well, well. No wonder you locked your bedroom door when you lived with us."

"That wasn't the only reason," she said before she thought.

His black eyes narrowed. "You've had a hell of a life, haven't you? And now this, on top of the past."

She bit her lower lip. "This door does have a lock?" she persisted. "I'm sorry. I've spent my life behind locked doors. It's a hard habit to break, and not because of the way I sleep."

"The door has a lock, and you can use it. But I hope you know that you're safe with me," he replied quietly. "Seducing innocents isn't a habit with me, and my men are trustworthy."

"It's not that."

"If you're nervous about being the only woman here, I could get Lisette to come over and spend the night in this room with you," he added.

"No," she said, reluctant to meet his paramour. "I'll be fine."

"You haven't been alone since it happened," he reminded her. "It may be more traumatic than you think, especially in the dark."

"I'll be all right, Micah," she said firmly.

He drew in an irritated breath. "All right. But if you're frightened, I'm next door, through the bathroom."

She gave him a curious look.

"I'll wear pajama bottoms while you're in residence," he said dryly, reading her mind accurately.

She cleared her throat. "Thanks."

"Don't you want to eat something before you go to bed?"

She shook her head. "I'm too tired. Micah, thanks for saving me. I didn't expect it, but I'm very grateful."

He shrugged. "You're family," he said flatly, and she grimaced when he wasn't looking. He turned and went out, hesitating before he closed the door. "Someone will be within shouting distance, night or day."

Her heart ached. He still didn't see her as a woman. Probably, he never would. "Okay," she replied. "Thanks."

He closed the door.

She was so tired that she was sure she'd be asleep almost as soon as her head connected with the pillow. But that wasn't the case. Dressed only in her cotton briefs, she lay awake for a long time, staring at the ceiling, absorbing the shock of the past two days. It seemed unreal now, here where she was safe. As her strung muscles began to relax, she tugged the cool, expensive designer sheet in a yellow rose pattern over her and felt her mind begin to drift slowly into peaceful oblivion.

"Callie? Callie!"

The deep forceful voice combined with steely fingers on her upper arms to shake her out of the nightmare she'd been having. She was hoarse from the scream that had dragged Micah from sleep and sent him running to the connecting door with a skeleton key.

She was sitting up, both her wrists in one of his lean, warm hands, her eyes wide with terror. She was shaking all over, and not from the air-conditioning.

He leaned over and turned on the bedside lamp. His eyes went helplessly to the full, high thrust of her tip-tilted little breasts, their nipples relaxed from sleep. She was so shaken that she didn't even feel embarrassment. Her pale blue eyes were wild with horror.

"You're safe, baby," he said gently. "It's all right."

"Micah!" came a shout from outside the bedroom door. It was Bojo, alert as usual to any odd noise.

"Callie just had a nightmare, Bojo. It's okay. Go back to bed!"

"Sure thing, boss."

Footsteps faded down the corridor.

"I was back in the chair, at Lopez's house. That man had the knife again, and he was cutting me," she choked. Her wild, frightened eyes met Micah's.

"You'll shoot me, if they try to take me and you can't stop them, right?" she asked in a hoarse whisper.

"Nobody is going to take you away from here by force," he said gently. "I promise. I can protect you on this island. It's why I brought you here in the first place."

She sighed and relaxed a little. "I'm being silly. It was the dream. It was so real, and I was scared to death, Micah! It all came back the minute I fell asleep!" She shivered. "Can't you hold me?" she asked huskily, her eyes on his muscular, hair-roughened chest. Looking at it made her whole body tingle. "Just for a minute?"

"Are you out of your mind?" he ground out.

She searched his eyes. He looked odd. "Why not?"

"Because..." His gaze fell to her breasts. They were hard-tipped now, visibly taut with desire. His jaw clenched. His hands on her wrists tightened roughly.

"Oh, for heaven's sake. I forgot! Sorry." She tried to cover herself, but his hands were relentless. She cleared her throat and grimaced. "That hurts," she complained on a nervous laugh, tugging at his hands. They loosened, but only a fraction.

"Did you take those pills I gave you to make you sleep?" he asked suddenly.

"Yes. But they didn't keep me asleep." She blinked. She smiled drowsily. She felt very uninhibited. He was looking at her breasts and she liked it. Her head fell back, because he hadn't turned her loose. His hands weren't bruising anymore, but they were holding her wrists firmly. She arched her back sensuously and watched the way his eyes narrowed and glittered on her breasts. She saw his body tense, and she gave a husky, wicked little laugh.

"You like looking at me there, don't you?" she asked, vaguely aware that she was being reckless.

He made a rough sound and met her eyes again. "Yes," he said flatly. "I like it."

"I wanted to take my clothes off for you when I was just sixteen," she confided absently as her tongue ran away with her. "I wanted you to see me. I ached all over when you looked at me that last Christmas. I wanted you to kiss me so hard that it would bruise my mouth. I wanted to unbutton your shirt and pull my dress down and let you hold me like that." She shivered helplessly at the images that rushed into her reeling mind. "You're so sexy, Micah," she whispered huskily. "So handsome. And I was just plain and my breasts were small, nothing like those beautiful, buxom women you always dated. I knew you'd never want me the way I wanted you."

He shook her gently. "Callie, for God's sake, hush!" he grated, his whole body tensing with desire at the imagery she was creating.

She was too relaxed from the sleeping pills to listen to warnings. She smiled lazily. "I never wanted anybody to touch me until then," she said softly. "Men always seemed repulsive to me. Did I ever tell you that my mother's last lover tried to seduce me? I ran from him and he knocked me down the stairs. I broke my arm. My mother said it was my fault. She took me back to the foster home. She said I was a troublemaker, and told lies about what happened."

"Dear God!" he exclaimed.

"So after that, I wore floppy old clothes and no makeup and pulled my hair back so I looked like the plainest old maid on earth, and I acted real tough. They left me alone. Then my mother married your dad," she added. "And I didn't have to be afraid anymore. Except it was worse," she murmured drowsily, "because I wanted you to touch me. But you didn't like me that way. You said I was a tramp, like my mother..."

"I didn't mean it," he ground out. "I was only trying to spare you more heartache. You were just a baby, and I was old enough to know better. It was the only way I knew to keep you at arm's length."

"You wanted my mother," she accused miserably.

"Never!" he said, and sounded utterly disgusted. "She was hard as nails, and her idea of femininity was complete control. She was the most mercenary human being I ever met."

Her pale blue eyes blinked as she searched his black ones curiously. "You said I was, too."

"You're not mercenary, honey," he replied quietly. "You never were."

She sighed, and her breasts rose and fell, drawing his attention again. "I feel so funny, Micah," she murmured.

"Funny, how?" he asked without thinking.

She laughed softly. "I don't know how to describe it. I feel...like I'm throbbing. I feel swollen."

She was describing sexual arousal, and he was fighting it like mad. He drew in a long, slow breath and forced himself to let go of her wrists. Her arms fell to her sides and he stared helplessly at the thrust of her small, firm breasts.

"It's so sad," she sighed. "The only time you've

ever looked at me or touched me was because I was hurt and needed medical attention.'' She laughed involuntarily.

''You have to stop this. Right now,'' he said firmly.

''Stop what?'' she asked with genuine curiosity.

He lifted the sheet and placed it over her breasts, pulling one of her hands up to hold it there.

She glowered at him as he got to his feet. ''That's great,'' she muttered. ''That's just great. Are you the guy at a striptease who yells 'put it back on'?''

He chuckled helplessly. ''Not usually, no. I'll leave the door between our rooms and the bathroom open. You can sing out if you get scared again.''

''Gosh, you're brave,'' she said. ''Aren't you afraid to leave your door unlocked? I might sneak in and ravish you in your sleep.''

''I wear a chastity belt,'' he said with a perfectly straight face.

Her eyes widened and suddenly she burst out laughing.

He grinned. ''That's more like it. Now lie back down and stop trying to seduce me. When you wake up and remember the things you've said and done tonight, you'll blush every time you look at me.''

She shrugged. ''I guess I will.'' She frowned. ''What was in those pills?''

''A sedative. Obviously it has an unpredictable reaction on you,'' he commented with a long, amused look. ''Either that or I've discovered a brand-new aphrodisiac. It makes retiring virgins wanton, apparently.''

She glared up at him. ''I am not wanton, and it wasn't my fault, anyway. I was very scared and you came running in here to flaunt your bare chest at me," she pointed out.

"You were the one doing the flaunting," he countered. "I'm going to have Lisette buy you some gowns, and while you're here, you'll wear them. I don't keep condoms handy anymore," he added bluntly.

She flushed and gasped audibly. "Micah Steele!" she burst out, horrified at the crude remark.

"Don't pretend you don't know what one is. You're not that naive. But that's the only way I'd ever have sex with you, even if I lost my head long enough to stifle my conscience," he added bluntly. "Because I don't want kids, or a wife, ever."

"I've already told you that I'm not proposing marriage!"

"You tried to seduce me," he accused.

"You tempted me! In fact, you drugged me!"

He was trying valiantly not to laugh. "I never!" he defended himself. "I gave you a mild sedative. A very mild sedative!"

"It was probably Spanish Fly," she taunted. "I've read about what it's supposed to do to women. You gave it to me deliberately so that I'd flash my breasts at you and make suggestive remarks, no doubt!"

He pursed his lips and lifted his chin, muffling laughter. "For the record, you've got gorgeous breasts," he told her. "But I've never seen myself as a tutor for a sensuous virgin. In case you were thinking along those lines."

She felt that compliment down to her toes and tried not to disgrace herself by showing it. Apparently he didn't think her breasts were too small at all. Imagine that! "There are lots of men who'd just love to have sex with me," she told him haughtily.

"What a shame that I'm the only one you'd submit to."

She glared at him. "Weren't you going back to bed?" she asked pointedly.

He sighed. "I might as well, if you're through undressing for me."

"I didn't undress for you! I sleep like this."

"I'll bet you didn't before you moved in with my father and me," he drawled softly.

Her flush was a dead giveaway.

"*And* you never locked your bedroom door at home," he added.

"For all the good it did me," she said grimly.

"I never got my kicks as a voyeur, especially with precocious teenagers," he told her. "You're much more desirable now, with a little age on you. Not," he added, holding up one lean hand, "that I have any plans to succumb. You're a picket-fence sort of woman."

"And you like yours in combat gear, with muscles," she retorted.

His eyes sketched her body under the sheet. "If I ever had the urge to marry," he said slowly, "you'd be at the top of my list of prospects, Callie. You're kindhearted and honest and brave. I was proud of you in the jungle."

She smiled. "Were you, really? I was terribly scared."

"All of us are, when we're being hunted. The trick is to keep going anyway." He pushed her down gently with the sheet up to her neck and her head on the pillow, and he tucked her in very gently. "Go back to sleep," he said, tracing a path down her cheek with a lean forefinger. He smiled. "You can dream about having wild sex with me."

"I don't have a clue about how to have wild sex," she pointed out. She lifted both eyebrows and her eyes twinkled as she gave him a wicked smile. "I'll bet you're great in bed."

"I am," he said without false modesty. "But," he added somberly, "you're a virgin. First times are painful and embarrassing, nothing like the torrid scenes in those romance novels you like to read."

She drew in a drowsy breath. "I figured that."

He had to get out of here. He was aroused already. It wouldn't take much to tempt him, and she'd been through enough already. He tapped her on the tip of her nose. "Sleep well."

"Micah, can I ask you something?" she murmured, blinking as she tried to stay awake.

"Go ahead."

"What did my mother see that made her think she'd enticed you that night we had the blowup?"

"Are you sure you want to know?" he asked. "Because if you do, I'll show you."

Her breath caught in her throat and her heart pounded. She looked at him with uninhibited curiosity and hunger. "I'm sure."

"Okay. Your choice." He unsnapped his pajama bottoms, and let them fall. "She saw this," he said quietly.

Her eyes went to that part of him that the pajamas had hidden. She wasn't so naive that she hadn't seen statues, and photographs in magazines, of naked men. But he sure didn't look like any of the pictures. There were no white lines on him anywhere. He was solid muscle, tanned and exquisitely male. Her eyes went helplessly to that part of him that was most male, and she almost gasped. He was impressive, even to an innocent.

"Do you understand what you're seeing, Callie?" he asked quietly.

"Yes," she managed in a husky whisper. "You're…you're aroused, aren't you?"

He nodded. "When I got away from you that Christmas night, I was like this, just from being close to you," he explained quietly, his voice strained. "The slacks I was wearing were tailored to fit properly, so it was noticeable. Your mother was experienced, and when she saw it, she thought it was because of her. She was wearing a strappy little silver dress, and she had an inflated view of her own charms. I found her repulsive."

"I didn't know men looked like that." Her lips parted as she continued to stare at him. "Are you…I mean, is that…normal?"

"I do occasionally inspire envy in other men," he murmured with a helpless laugh. He pulled his pajama trousers back up and snapped them in place, almost shivering with the hunger to throw himself down on top of her and ravish her. She had no idea of the effect that wide-eyed curiosity had on him. "Now I'm getting out of here before it gets any worse!" he said in a tight voice. "Good night."

She stretched, feeling oddly swollen and achy. She stretched, feeling unfamiliar little waves of pleasure washing over her at the intimacy they'd just shared. She noticed that his face went even tauter as he watched her stretch. It felt good. But she was really sleepy and her eyelids felt heavy. Her eyes began to close. "Gosh, I'm tired. I think I can sleep...now." Her voice trailed off as she sighed heavily and her whole body relaxed in the first stages of sleep.

He looked at her with pure temptation. She'd been sedated, of course, or she'd never have been so uninhibited with him. He knew that, but it didn't stop the frustrated desire he felt from racking his powerful body.

"I'm so glad that one of us can sleep," he murmured with icy sarcasm, but she was already asleep. He gave her one last, wistful stare, and went out of the room quickly.

The next morning, Callie awoke after a long and relaxing sleep feeling refreshed. Then she remembered what had happened in the middle of the night and she was horrified.

She searched through the bag Micah's friend had packed for her, looking for something concealing and unnoticeable, but there wasn't a change of clothing. She only had the jeans and shirt she'd been wearing the day before. Grimacing, she put them back on and ran a brush through her short dark hair. She didn't bother with makeup at all.

When she went into the kitchen, expecting to find it empty, Micah was going over several sheets of paper with a cup of black coffee in one big hand. He gave her a quick glance and watched the blush cover her high cheekbones. His lean, handsome face broke into a wicked grin

"Good morning," he drawled. "All rested, are we? Ready for another round of show and tell?"

She ground her teeth together and avoided looking directly at him as she poured herself a cup of coffee from the coffeemaker on the counter and added creamer to it.

"I was drugged!" she said defensively, sitting down at the table. She couldn't make herself look him in the eye.

"Really?"

"You should know," she returned curtly. "You drugged me!"

"I gave you a mild sedative," he reminded her. He gave her a mischievous glance. "But I'll be sure to remember the effects."

She cleared her throat and sipped her coffee. "Can you find me something to do around here?" she asked. "I'm not used to sitting around doing nothing."

"I phoned Lisse about thirty minutes ago," he said. "She'll be over at ten to take you shopping."

"So soon?" she asked curiously.

"You don't have a change of clothes, do you?" he asked.

She shook her head. "No."

"Maddie travels light and expects everyone else to, as well," he explained. "Especially in tight corners. I'll give you my credit card..."

"I have my own with my passport," she said at once, embarrassed. "Thanks, but I pay my own way."

"So you said." He eyed her over his coffee cup. "I won't expect anything in return," he added. "In case that thought crossed your mind."

"I know that. But I don't want to be obligated to you any more than I already am."

"You sound like me, at your age," he mused. "I

never liked to accept help, either. But we all come to it, Callie, sooner or later.''

She let out a slow breath and sipped more coffee. ''I couldn't repay you in a hundred years for what you did for me,'' she said gently. ''You risked your life to get me out of there.''

''All in a day's work, honey,'' he said, and smiled. ''Besides,'' he added, ''I had a score to settle with Lopez.'' His face hardened. ''I've got an even bigger one to settle, now. I have to put him out of action, before he organizes his men and goes after Dad!''

## *Chapter Seven*

Callie felt her heart go cold at the words. She'd been through so much herself that she'd forgotten briefly that Jack Steele was in danger, too. Micah had said that Pogo and Maddie would watch over him, but obviously he still had fears.

"You don't think he'll be safe with your people?" she asked worriedly.

"Not if Lopez gets his act together," he said coolly. "Which is why I've had Bojo send him a message in the clear, rubbing it in that I took you away from him."

She felt uneasy. "Isn't that dangerous, with a man like Lopez?"

"Very," he agreed. "But if he's concentrating on me, he's less likely to expend his energy on Dad. Right?"

"Right," she agreed. "What do you want me to do?"

He lowered his eyes to his coffee cup and lifted it to his chiseled mouth. "You do whatever you like. You're here as my guest."

She frowned. "I don't need a holiday, Micah."

"You're getting one, regardless. Today you can go shopping with Lisse. Tomorrow, I'll take you sight-seeing, if you like."

"Is it safe?"

He chuckled. "We won't be alone," he pointed out. "I intend taking Bojo and Peter and Rodrigo along with us."

"Oh."

"Disappointed?" he asked with faint arrogance. "Would you rather be alone with me, on a deserted beach?"

She glared at him. "You stop that."

"Spoilsport. You do rise to the bait so beautifully." He leaned back in his chair and the humor left his eyes. "Bojo's going with you to Nassau. Buy what you like, but make sure you don't bring home low-cut blouses and short-shorts or short skirts. There aren't any other women on this island, except a couple of married middle-aged island women who live with their husbands and families. I don't want anything to divert the men's attention with Lopez on the loose."

"I don't wear suggestive clothing," she pointed out.

"You do around me," he said flatly. "Considering last night's showing, I thought the warning might be appropriate."

"I was drugged!" she repeated, flushing.

"I don't mind if you show your body to me," he continued, as if she hadn't spoken. "I enjoy looking at it. But I'm not sharing the sight. Besides, for the next week or two, you're my sister. I don't want anyone speculating about our exact relationship."

"Why? Because of your friend Lisette?" she asked bitterly.

"Exactly," he said with a poker face. "Lisette and I are lovers," he added bluntly. "The last thing I need is a jealous tug-of-war in a crisis."

She caught her breath audibly. It was cruel of him to say such a thing. Or maybe he was being cruel to be kind, making sure that she didn't get her hopes up.

She lifted her head with postured arrogance. "That's wishful thinking," she said firmly. "I know you're terribly disappointed that I haven't proposed, but you'd better just deal with it."

For an instant he looked shocked, then he laughed. It occurred to him that he'd never laughed as much in his life as he had with her, especially the past couple of days. Considering the life or death situation they'd been in, it was even more incredible. Callie was a real mate under fire. He'd heard stories about wives of retired mercs walking right into fire with their husbands. He'd taken them with a grain of salt until he'd seen Callie in a more desperate situation than any of those wives had ever been in.

"You made me proud, in Cancún," he said after a minute. "Really proud. If we had campfires, you're the sort of woman we'd build into legend around them."

She flushed. "Like Maddie?"

"Maddie's never been in the situation you were

in," he said somberly. "I don't even know another woman who has. Despite the nightmares, you held up as well as any man I've ever served with."

She smiled slowly. "A real compliment, wow," she murmured. "If you'll write all that down, I'll have it notarized and hang it behind my desk. Mr. Kemp will be very impressed."

He glowered at her. "Kemp's more likely to hang you on the wall beside it. You're wasted in a law office."

"I love what I do," she protested. "I dig out little details that save lives and careers. Law isn't dry and boring, it's alive. It's history."

"It's a job in a little hick Texas town while you'll eventually dry up and blow away like a sun-scorched creosote bush."

She searched his dark eyes. "That's how it felt to you, I know. You never liked living in Jacobsville. But I'm not like you," she added softly. "I want a neat little house with a flower garden and neighbors to talk to over the fence, and a couple of children." Her face softened as she thought about it. "Not right away, of course. But someday."

"Just the thought of marriage gives me chest pain," he said with veiled contempt. "More often than not, a woman marries for money and a man marries for sex. What difference does a sheet of paper with signatures make?"

"If you have to ask, you wouldn't understand the answer," she said simply. "I guess you don't want kids."

He frowned. He'd never thought about having kids. It was one of those "someday" things he didn't give much time to. He studied Callie and pictured her again with a baby in her arms. It was surprisingly nice.

"It would be hard to carry a baby through jungle undergrowth with a rifle under one arm," she answered her own question. "And in your line of work, I don't suppose leaving a legacy to children is much of a priority."

He averted his head. "I expect to spend what I make while I'm still alive," he said.

She looked out over the bay, her eyes narrowing in the glare of the sunlight. The casuarinas lining the beach were towering and their feathery fronds waved gracefully in the breeze that always blew near the water. Flowers bloomed everywhere. The sand was like sugar, white and picturesque.

"It's like a living travel poster," she remarked absently. "I've never seen water that color except in postcards, and I thought it was just a bad color job."

"There are places in the Pacific and the Caribbean like it," he told her. He glanced toward the pier as he heard the sound of a motor. "There's Lisse," he said. "Come and be introduced."

She got up and followed along behind him, feeling like a puppy that couldn't be left alone. As she watched, a gorgeous blonde in a skimpy yellow sundress with long legs and long hair let Micah help her onto the pier. Unexpectedly he jerked her against him and kissed her so passionately that Callie flushed and looked away in embarrassment. He was obviously terrified that she might read something into last night, so he was making his relationship with Lisse very plain.

A few minutes later, Micah put something into Lisse's hand and spoke softly to her. Lisse laughed breathily and said something that Callie couldn't hear. Micah took the blonde by the hand and led her down the pier to where Callie was waiting at a respectful distance.

Up close, the blonde had a blemishless complexion and perfect teeth. She displayed them in a smile that would do credit to a supermodel, which was what the woman really looked like.

"I'm Lisette Dubonnet, but everyone calls me Lisse," she introduced herself and held out a hand to firmly shake Callie's.

"I'm Callie…" she began.

"My sister," Micah interrupted, obviously not trusting her to play along. "She's taking a holiday from her job in Texas. I want you to help her buy some leisure wear. Her suitcase didn't arrive with her."

"Oh," Lisse said, and laughed. "I've had that happen. I know *just* how you feel. Well, shall we go? Micah, are you coming with us?"

Micah shook his head. "I've got things to do here, but Bojo wants to come along, if you don't mind. He has to check on a package his brother is sending over from Georgia."

"He's perfectly welcome," Lisse said carelessly. "Come along, Callie. Callie…what a pretty name. A little rare, I should say."

"It's short for Colleen," Callie told her, having to almost run to keep up with the woman's long strides.

"We'll go downtown in Nassau. There are lots of chic little boutiques there. I'm sure we can find something that will do for you."

"You're very kind…"

Lisse held up an imperative hand as they reached

the boat she'd just disembarked from. "It's no bother. Micah never speaks of you. Did he have you hidden in a closet or something?"

"We don't get along very well," Callie formulated. It was the truth, too, mostly.

"And that's very odd. Micah gets along wonderfully with most women."

"But then you're not related to him," Callie pointed out, just managing to clamber aboard the boat before the line was untied by Bojo, who was already there and waiting to leave.

"No, thank God I'm not." Lisse laughed. Even her laugh was charming. "I'd kill myself. Hurry up, Bojo, Dad and I have to go to an embassy ball tonight, so I'm pressed for time!"

"I am coming, mademoiselle!" he said with a grin and leaped down into the boat.

"Let's go, Marchand!" she called to the captain, who replied respectfully and turned the expensive speedboat back into the bay and headed it toward Nassau.

"We could postpone this trip, if you don't have time," Callie offered.

"Not necessary," Lisse said. "I'll have less time later on. I try to do anything Micah asks me to. He's always *so* grateful," she added in a purring tone.

And I can just imagine what form that takes, Callie thought, but she didn't say it. Even so, Bojo heard their conversation, caught Callie's eye, and grinned so wickedly that she cleared her throat and asked Lisse about the history of Nassau to divert her.

Nassau was bustling with tourists. The colorful straw market at the docks was doing a booming business, and fishing boats rocked gently on the waves made by passing boats. Seagulls made passes at the water and flew gracefully past the huge glass windows of the restaurant that sat right on the bay. It was beautiful. Just beautiful. Callie, who'd never been anywhere—well, except for the road trip to Cancún with the drug lord's minions while she was unconscious—thought it was pure delight.

"Don't gawk like a tourist, darling," Lisse scoffed as they made their way past the fishing boats and into an arcade framed in an antique stone arch covered in bougainvillea. "It's only Nassau."

But Callie couldn't help it. She loved the musical accents she caught snatches of as they strolled past shops featuring jewelry with shell motifs and handcrafts from all over Europe, not to mention dress shops and T-shirt shops galore. She loved the stone pathways and the flowers that bloomed everywhere. They went past a food stand and her nose wrinkled.

"I thought I smelled liquor," she said under her breath.

"You did," Lisse said nonchalantly, waving her painted fingernails in the general direction of the counter. "You can buy any sort of alcoholic drink you want at any of these food stands."

"It's legal?"

"Of course it's legal. Haven't you been anywhere?"

Callie smiled sheepishly. "Not really. Now this is the sort of shop I need," she said suddenly, stopping at a store window displaying sundresses, jeans and T-shirts and sneakers. It also displayed the cards it accepted, and Callie had one of them. "I'll only be a minute..."

"Darling, not there!" Lisse lamented. "It's one of those cheap touristy shops! Micah wants you to use his charge card. I've got it in my pocket. He wants you to wear things that won't embarrass him." She put her fingers over her mouth. "Oh, dear, I forgot, I wasn't to tell you that he said that." She grimaced. "Well, anyway…"

"Well, anyway," Callie interrupted, following Lisse's lead, "this is where I'm shopping, with *my* card. You can wait or come in. Suit yourself."

She turned and left Lisse standing there with her mouth gaping, and she didn't care. The woman was horrible!

After she'd tried on two pairs of jeans, two sundresses, a pair of sandals, one of sneakers and four T-shirts, she felt guilty for the way she'd talked to Micah's woman. But Lisse was hard-going, especially after that kiss she'd witnessed. It had hurt right to the bone, and Lisse's condescending, snappy attitude didn't endear her to Callie, either.

She came back out of the shop with two bags. "Thank you very much. I'd like to go back to the house, now," she told Lisse, and she didn't smile.

Lisse made a moue with her perfect mouth. "I've hurt your feelings. I'm sorry. But Micah told me what to do. He'll be furious with me now."

What a pity. She didn't say it. "He can be furious with me," Callie said, walking ahead of Lisse back the way they'd come. "I buy my own clothes and pay my own way. I'm not a helpless parasite. I don't need a man to buy things for me."

There was a stony silence from behind her. She stopped and turned and said, "Oh, my, did I hurt your feelings? I'm sorry." And with a wicked gleam in her eyes at the other woman's furious flush, she walked back toward the boat.

Bojo knew something was going on, but he was too polite to question Lisse's utter silence all the way back to the pier. He got out first to tie up the boat and reached down to help Callie out, relieving her of her packages on the way. Micah had heard the boat and was strolling down the pier to meet them. There was a scramble as Lisse climbed out of the boat, cursing her captain for not being quick enough to spare her a stumble. She sounded like she was absolutely seething!

"We'd better run for it," Callie confided to Bojo.

"What did you do?" he asked under his breath.

"I called her a parasite. I think she's upset."

He muffled a laugh, nodded respectfully at his boss and herded Callie down the pier at very nearly a run while Micah stood staring after them with a scowl. Seconds later Lisse reached him and her voice carried like a bullhorn.

"She's got the breeding of a howler monkey, and the dress sense of an octopus!" she raged. "I wouldn't take her to the nearest tar pit without a bribe!"

Callie couldn't help it. She broke down and ran even faster, with Bojo right beside her.

Later, of course, she had to face the music. She'd changed into a strappy little blue-and-white-striped sundress. It was ankle-length with a square bodice and wide shoulder straps. Modest even enough for her surroundings. She was barefoot, having disliked the fit of the sandals she'd bought that rubbed against her big toe. Micah came striding toward her where she was lounging under a sea grape tree watching the fishing boats come into the harbor.

Micah was in cutoff denims that left his long, powerful legs bare, and he was wearing an open shirt. His chest was broad and hair-roughened and now Callie couldn't look at it without feeling it under her hands.

"Can't you get along with anyone?" he demanded, his fists on his narrow hips as he glared down at her.

"My boss Mr. Kemp thinks I'm wonderful," she countered.

His eyes narrowed. "You gave Lisse fits, and she only came over to do you a favor, when she was already pressed for time."

Her eyebrows arched over shimmering blue eyes. "You don't think I'm capable of walking into a shop and buying clothes all by myself? Whatever sort of women are you used to?"

"And you called her a parasite," he added angrily.

"Does she work?"

He hesitated. "She's her father's hostess."

"I didn't ask you about her social life, I asked if she worked for her living. She doesn't. And she said that when she did you favors, you repaid her handsomely." She cocked her head up at him. "I suppose, in a pinch, you could call that working for her living. But it isn't a profession I'd want to confess to in public."

He just stood there, scowling.

"I make my own living," she continued, "and pay my own way. I don't rely on men to support me, buy me clothes, or chauffeur me around."

"Lisse is used to a luxurious lifestyle," he began slowly, but without much conviction.

"I'm sure that I've misjudged her," she said placatingly. "Why, if you lost everything tomorrow, I know she'd be the first person to rush to your side and offer to help you make it all back with hard work."

He pursed his lips and thought about that.

"That's what I thought," she said sweetly.

He was glaring again. "I told you to put everything on my card, and get nice things."

"You told Lisse to take me to expensive dress shops so that I wouldn't buy cheap stuff and embarrass you," she countered, getting to her feet. She brushed off her skirt, oblivious to the shocked look on his face, before she lifted her eyes back to his. "I don't care if I embarrass you," she pointed out bluntly. "You can always hide me in a closet when you have guests if you're ashamed of me."

He made a rough sound. "You'd walk right into the living room and tell them why you were hidden."

She shrugged. "Blame it on a rough childhood. I don't like people pushing me around. Especially model-type parasites."

"Lisse is not—" he started.

"I don't care what she is or isn't," she cut him off, "she's not bossing me around and insulting me!"

"What did you tell her about our relationship?" he demanded, and he was angry.

"I told her nothing," she countered hotly. "It's none of her business. But, for the record, if you really were my brother, I'd have you stuffed and mounted and I'd use you for an ashtray!"

She walked right past him and back into the house. She heard muffled curses, but she didn't slow down. Let him fume. She didn't care.

She didn't come out for supper. She sat in a peacock chair out on the patio overlooking the bay and enjoyed the delicious floral smell of the musty night air in the delicious breeze, while sipping a piña colada. She'd never had one and she was curious about the taste, so she'd had Mac fix her one, along with a sandwich. She wasn't really afraid of Micah, but she was hoping to avoid him until they both cooled down.

He came into her room without knocking and walked right out onto the patio. He was wearing a tuxedo with a faintly ruffled fine white cotton shirt, and he looked so handsome that her heart stopped and fluttered at just the sight of him.

"Are you going to a funeral, or did you get a job as a waiter?" she asked politely.

He managed not to laugh. It wasn't funny. She wasn't funny. She'd insulted Lisse and the woman was going to give him fits all night. "I'm taking Lisse to an embassy ball," he said stiffly. "I would have invited you, but you don't have anything to wear," he added with a vicious smile.

"Just as well," she murmured, lifting her glass to him in a mock toast. "It would have blood all over it by the end of the night, if I'm any judge of miffed women."

"Lisse is a lady," he said shortly. "Something you have no concept of, with your ignorance of proper manners."

That hurt, but she smiled. "Blame it on a succession of foster homes," she told him sweetly. "Manners aren't a priority."

He hated being reminded of the life she'd led. It made him feel guilty, and he didn't like it. "Pity," he said scathingly. "You might consider taking lessons."

"I always think that if you're going to fight, you should get down in the mud and roll around, not use words."

"Just what I'd expect from a little savage like you," he said sarcastically.

The word triggered horrible memories. She reacted to it out of all proportion, driven by her past. She leaped to her feet, eyes blazing, the glass trembling in her hand. "One more word, and you'll need a shower and a dry cleaner to get out the door!"

"Don't you like being called a savage?" He lifted his chin as her hand drew back. "You wouldn't daaa....re!"

He got it right in the face. It didn't stay there. It dribbled down onto his spotless white shirt and made little white trickles down over his immaculate black tuxedo.

She frowned. "Damn. I forgot the toast." She lifted the empty glass at him. *"Salud y pesetas!"* she said in Spanish, with a big furious smile. Health and wealth.

His fists clenched at his sides. He didn't say a word. He didn't move a muscle. He just looked at her with those black eyes glittering like a coiling cobra.

She wiggled her eyebrows. "It will be an adventure. Lisse can lick it off! Think of the new experiences you can share...now, Micah,'' she shifted gears and started backing up.

He was moving. He was moving very slowly, very deliberately, with the steps of a man who didn't care if he had to go to jail for homicide. She noticed that at once.

She backed away from him. He really did look homicidal. Perhaps she'd gone a little too far. Her mouth tended to run away from her on good days, even when she wasn't insulted and hadn't had half a glass of potent piña colada to boot. She wasn't used to alcohol at all.

''Let's be reasonable,'' she tried. She was still backing up. ''I do realize that I might have overreacted. I'll apologize.''

He kept coming.

''I'm really sorry,'' she tried again, holding up both hands, palms toward him, as if to ward him off.

He still kept coming.

''And I promise, faithfully, that I will never do it...*aaaaahh!*''

There was a horrific splash and she swallowed half the swimming pool. She came up soaked, sputtering, freezing, because the water was cold. She clamored over the softly lit water to the concrete edge and grabbed hold of the ladder to pull herself up. It was really hard, because her full skirt was soaked and heavy.

''Like hell you do,'' he said fiercely, and started to push her back in.

She was only trying to save herself. But she grabbed his arms and overbalanced him, and he went right into the pool with her, headfirst.

This time when she got to the surface, he was right beside her. His black eyes were raging now.

She pushed her hair out of her eyes and mouth. "I'm *really* sorry," she panted.

He was breathing deliberately. "Would you like to explain why you went ballistic for no reason?" he demanded.

She grimaced, treading water and trying not to sink. She couldn't swim *very well.* She was ashamed of her behavior, but the alcohol had loosened all her inhibitions. She supposed she owed him the truth. She glanced at him and quickly away again. "When that man hit on me and made me break my arm, he told my mother I was a lying little savage and that I needed to be put away. That's when my mother took me back to my foster family and disowned me," she bit off the words, averting her eyes.

There was a long silence. He swam to the ladder, waiting for her to join him. But she was tired and cold and emotionally drained. And when she tried to dog-paddle, her arms were just too tired. She sank.

Powerful arms caught her, easing her to the surface effortlessly so that she could breathe. He sat her on the edge and climbed out, reaching down to lift her out beside him. He took her arm and led her back up the cobblestoned walkway to the patio.

"I can pack and go home tomorrow," she offered tautly.

"You can't leave," he said flatly. "Lopez knows where you are."

She lifted her weary eyes to his hard, cold face. "Poor you," she said. "Stuck with me."

His eyes narrowed. "You haven't dealt with any

of it, have you?'' he asked quietly. ''You're still carrying your childhood around on your back.''

''We all do, to some extent,'' she said with a long sigh. ''I'm sorry I ruined your suit. I'm sorry I was rude to Lisse. I'll apologize, if you like,'' she added humbly.

''You don't like her.''

She shrugged. ''I don't know her. I just don't have a high opinion of women who think money is what life is all about.''

He scowled. ''What *is* it all about?'' he challenged.

She searched his eyes slowly. ''Pain,'' she said in a husky tone, and she winced involuntarily before she could stop herself. ''I'm going to bed. Good night.''

She was halfway in the door when he called her back.

She didn't turn. ''Yes?''

He hesitated. He wanted to apologize, he really did. But he didn't know how. He couldn't remember many regrets.

She laughed softly to herself. ''I know. You wish you'd never been landed with me. You might not believe it, but so do I.''

''If you'll give me the name of the shop where you bought that stuff, I'll have them transfer it to my account.''

''Fat chance, Steele,'' she retorted as she walked away.

# Chapter Eight

After a restless night, but thankfully with no nightmares, Callie put on a colorful sundress and went out onto the beach barefoot to pick up shells. She met Bojo on the way. He was wearing the long oyster silk hooded djellaba she'd never seen him out of.

He gave her a rueful glance. "The boss had to send to town for a new tuxedo last night," he said with twinkling dark eyes. "I understand you took him swimming."

She couldn't help chuckling. "I didn't mean to. We had a name-calling contest and he lost."

He chuckled, too. "You know, his women rarely accost him. They fawn over him, play up to him, stroke his ego and live for expensive presents."

"I'm his sister," she said neutrally.

"You are not," he replied gently. He smiled at her surprised glance. "He does occasionally share things with me," he added. "I believe the fiction is to protect you from Lisse. She is obsessively jealous of him and not a woman to make an enemy of. She has powerful connections and little conscience."

"Oh, I got to her before I got to him, if you recall," Callie said with a wry glance. She scuffed her toes in the sand, unearthing part of a perfect shell. She bent to pick it up. "I guess I'll be fish food if she has mob connections."

He chuckled. "I wouldn't rule that out, but you are safe enough here," he admitted. "What are you doing?"

"Collecting shells to take back home," she said, her eyes still on the beach. "I've lived inland all my life. I don't think I've ever even seen the ocean. Galveston is on the bay, and it isn't too far from Jacobsville, but I've never been there, either. It just fascinates me!" She glanced at him. "Micah said you were from Morocco. That's where the Sahara Desert is, isn't it?"

"Yes, but I am from Tangier. It is far north of the desert."

"But it's desert, too, isn't it?" she wondered.

He laughed pleasantly. "Tangier is a seaport, mademoiselle. In fact, it looks a lot like Nassau. That's why I don't mind working here with Micah."

"Really?" She just stared at him. "Isn't it funny, how we get mental pictures of faraway places, and they're nothing like what you see when you get there? I've seen postcards of the Bahamas, but I thought that water was painted, because it didn't even look real. But it is. It's the most astonishing group of colors..."

"Bojo!"

He turned to see his boss coming toward them, taciturn and threatening. It was enough for Callie to hear the tone of his voice to know that he was angry. She didn't turn around, assuming he had chores for Bojo.

"See you," she said with a smile.

He lifted both eyebrows. "I wonder," he replied enigmatically, and went down the beach to speak to Micah.

Minutes later, Micah strolled down the beach where Callie was kneeling and sorting shells damp with seawater and coated with sand. He was wearing sand-colored slacks with casual shoes and an expensive silk shirt under a sports coat. He looked elegant and so handsome that Callie couldn't continue looking at him without letting her admiration show.

"Are you here for an apology?" she asked, concentrating on the shells instead of him. Her heart was pounding like mad, but at least her voice sounded calm.

There was a pause. "I'm here to take you sightseeing."

Her heart jumped. She'd thought that would be the last thing on his mind after their argument the night before. She glanced at his knees and away again. "Thanks for the offer, but I'd rather hunt shells, if it's all the same to you."

He stuck his hands into his pockets and glared at her dark, bent head, his mouth making a thin line in a hard face. He felt guilty about the things he'd said to her the night before, and she'd made him question his whole lifestyle with that remark about Lisse. When he looked back, he had to admit that most of the women in his life had been out for material rewards. Far from looking for love, they'd been looking for expensive jewelry, nights out in the fanciest nightclubs and restaurants, sailing trips on his yacht. Callie wouldn't even let him buy her a decent dress.

He glared at the dress she was wearing with bridled fury. Lisse had spent the evening condemning Callie for everything from her Texas accent to her lack of style. It had been one of the most unpleasant dates of his life, and when he'd refused her offer to stay the night at her apartment, she'd made furious comments about his "unnatural" attraction to his sister. Rather than be accused of perversion, he'd been forced to tell the truth. That had only made matters worse. Lisse had stormed into her apartment house without a word and he knew that she was vindictive. He'd have to watch Callie even more carefully now.

"I guess she gave you hell all night, huh?" Callie asked his shoes. "I'm really sorry."

He let out a harsh breath. His dark eyes went to the waves caressing the white sand near the shore. Bits of seaweed washed up over the occasional shell, along with bits of palm leaves.

"Why don't you want to see Nassau?"

She stood up and lifted one of her bare feet. There was a noticeable blister between her big toe and the next one, on both feet. "Because I'd have to go barefoot. I got the wrong sort of sandals. They've got a thong that goes between your toes, and I'm not used to them. Sneakers don't really go with this dress."

"Not much would," he said with a scathing scrutiny of it. "Half the women on New Providence are probably wearing one just like it."

She glared at him. "Assembly line dresses are part of my lifestyle. I have to live within my means," she said with outraged pride. "I'm sorry if I don't dress up to your exacting standards, but I can't afford haute couture on take-home pay of a little over a hundred and fifty dollars a week!" Her chin tilted with even more hostility. "So spare your blushes and leave me to my shells. I'd hate to embarrass you by wearing my 'rags' out in public."

"Oh, hell!" he burst out, eyes flashing.

He was outraged, but she knew she'd hit the nail on the head. He didn't even try to pretend that he wasn't ashamed to take her out in public. "Isn't it better if I stay here, anyway? Surely I'm safer in a camp of armed men that I would be running around Nassau."

"You seem to be surgically attached to Bojo lately," he said angrily.

She lifted both eyebrows. "I like Bojo," she said. "He doesn't look down on the way I dress, or make fun of my accent, or ignore me when I'm around."

He was almost vibrating with anger. He couldn't remember any woman in his life making him as explosively angry as Callie could.

"Why don't you take Lisse sight-seeing?" she suggested, moving away from him. "You could start with the most expensive jeweler in Nassau and work your way to the most expensive boutique...Micah!"

He had her up in his arms and he was heading for the ocean.

She pushed at his broad chest. "Don't you dare, don't...you...dare, Micah!"

It didn't work. He swung her around and suddenly was about to toss her out right into the waves when the explosion came. There was a ricochet that was unmistakable to Micah, and bark flew off a palm tree nearby. "Bojo!" Micah yelled.

The other man, who was still within shouting distance, came running with a small weapon in his hands. Out beyond the breakers, there was a ship, a yacht, moving slowly. A glint of sunlight reflecting off metal was visible on the deck and the ricocheting sound came again.

"What the…!" she exclaimed, as Micah ran down the beach with her in his arms.

"This way!" Bojo yelled to him, and a sharp, metallic ripple of gunfire sounded somewhere nearby.

The firing brought other men to the beach, one of whom had a funny-looking long tube. It was Peter. Bojo called something to him. He protested, but Bojo insisted. He knelt, resting the tube on his shoulder, sighted and pulled the trigger. A shell flew out of it with a muffled roar. Seconds later, there was a huge splash in the water just off the yacht's bow.

"That'll buy us about a minute. Let's go!" Micah grabbed Callie up in his arms and rushed up the beach to the house at a dead run. His men stopped firing and followed. Micah called something to Bojo in a language Callie had never heard before.

"What was that?" she asked, shocked when he put her down inside the house. "What happened?"

"Lopez happened, unless I miss my guess. I was careless. It won't happen twice," Micah said flatly. He walked away while she was still trying to form questions.

Moments later, Micah went to find Bojo.

"The yacht is gone now, of course," Bojo said

angrily. "Peter is upset that I refused to let him blow her up."

"Some things require more authority than I have, even here," Micah said flatly. "But don't think I wasn't tempted to do just that. Lopez knows I have Callie, and he knows where she is now. He'll make a try for her." He looked at Bojo. "She can't be out of our sight again, not for a second."

"I am aware of that," the other man replied. His dark eyes narrowed. "Micah, does she have any idea at all that you're using her as bait?"

"If you so much as mention that to her…!" Micah threatened softly.

"I would not," he assured the older man. "But you must admit, it hardly seems the action of someone who cares for her."

Micah stared him down. "She's part of my family and I'll take care of her. But she's only part of my family because my father married her tramp of a mother. She's managed to endear herself to my father and it would kill him if anything happened to her," he said in a cold tone. "I can't let Lopez get to my father. Using Callie to bait him here, where I can deal with him safely, is the only way I have to get him at all, and I'm not backing down now!"

"As you wish," Bojo said heavily. "At least she has no idea of this."

Micah agreed. Neither of them saw the shadow at the door behind them retreat to a distance.

Callie went back to her room and closed the door very quietly before she let the tears roll down her white face. She'd have given two years of her life not to have heard those cold words from Micah's lips. She knew he was angry with her, but she didn't realize the contempt with which he was willing to risk her life, just to get Lopez. All he'd said about protecting her, keeping her safe, not letting Lopez get to her—it was all lies. He wanted her for bait. That was all she meant to him. He was doing it to save his father from Lopez, not to save her. Apparently she was expendable. Nothing in her life had ever hurt quite so much.

She seemed to go numb from the pain. She didn't feel anything, except emptiness. She sat down in the chair beside the window and looked out over the ocean. The ship that had been there was gone now, but Lopez knew where the house was, and how well it was guarded. Considering his record, she didn't imagine that he'd give up his quest just because Micah had armed men. Lopez had armed men, too, and all sorts of connections. He also had a reputation for never getting bested by anyone. He would do everything in his power to get Callie back, thinking Micah really cared for her. After all, he'd rescued her hadn't he?

She wrapped her arms around herself, remembering how it had been at Lopez's house, how that henchman had tortured her. She felt sick all over. This was even worse than being in the foster care system. She was all alone. There was no one to offer her protection, to comfort her, to value her. Her whole life had been like that. For just a little while, she'd had some wild idea that she mattered to Micah. What a joke.

At least she knew the truth now, even if she'd had to eavesdrop to learn it. She could only depend on herself. She was going to ask Bojo for a gun and get him to teach her to shoot it. If she had to fend for herself, and apparently she did, she wanted a chance for survival. Micah would probably turn her over to Lopez if he got a guarantee that Lopez would leave his father alone, she reasoned irrationally. The terror she felt was so consuming that she felt her whole body shaking with it.

When Micah opened the door to her room, she had to fight not to rage at him. It wasn't his fault that he didn't care for her, she told herself firmly. And she loved his father as much as he did. She managed to look at him without flinching, but the light in her eyes had gone out. They were quiet, haunted eyes with no life in them at all.

Micah saw that and frowned. She was different. "What's wrong? You're safe," he assured her. "Lopez was only letting us know he's nearby. Believe me, if he'd wanted you dead, you'd be dead."

She swallowed. "I figured that out," she said in a subdued tone. "What now?"

The frown deepened. "We wait, of course. He'll make another move. We'll draw back and let him think we didn't take the threat seriously. That will pull him in."

She lifted her eyes to his face. "Why don't you let me go sight-seeing alone?" she offered. "That would probably do the trick."

"And risk letting him take you again?" he asked solemnly.

She laughed without humor and turned her eyes back to the ocean. "Isn't that what you have in mind already?"

The silence behind her was arctic. "Would you like to explain that question?"

"In ancient times, when they wanted to catch a

lion, they tethered a live kid goat to a post and baited him with it. If the goat lived, they turned him loose, but if the lion got him, it didn't really matter. I mean, what's a goat more or less?''

Micah had never felt so many conflicting emotions at the same time. Foremost of them was shame. "You heard me talking to Bojo?''

She nodded.

His indrawn breath was the only sound in the room. "Callie,'' he began, without knowing what he could say to repair the damage.

"It's okay,'' she said to the picture window. "I never had any illusions about where I fit in your family. I still don't.''

His teeth ground together. Why should it be so painful to hear her say that? She was the interloper. She and her horrible mother had destroyed his relationship with his own father. He was alone because of her, so why should he feel guilty? But he did. He felt guilty and ashamed. He hadn't really meant everything he'd said to Bojo. Somewhere there was a vague jealousy of the easy friendship she had with his right-hand man, with the tenderness she gave Bojo, when she fought Micah tooth and nail.

"I'll do whatever you want me to,'' she said after a minute. "But I want a gun, and I want to learn how to use it.'' She stood up and turned to face him, defiant in the shark-themed white T-shirt and blue jeans she'd changed into. "Because if Lopez gets me this time, he's getting a dead woman. I'll never go through that again.''

Micah actually winced. "He's not getting you,'' he said curtly.

"Better me than Dad," she said with a cold smile. "Right?"

He slammed the door and walked toward her. She didn't even try to back up. She glared at him from a face that was tight with grief and misery, the tracks of tears still visible down her cheeks.

"Do you actually think I'd let him take you, even to save Dad?" he demanded furiously. "What sort of man do you think I am?"

"I have no idea," she said honestly. "You're a stranger. You always have been."

He searched her blue eyes with irritation and impatience. "You're a prime example of the reason I prefer mercenary women," he said without thinking. "You're nothing but a pain in the neck."

"Thank you. I love compliments."

"You probably thrive on insults," he bit off. Then he remembered how she'd had to live all those years, and could have slapped himself for taunting her.

"If they're all you ever hear, you get used to them," she agreed without rancor. "I'm tough. I've had to be. So do your worst, Micah," she added. "Tie me to a palm tree and wait in ambush for Lopez to shoot at me, I don't care."

But she did care. There was real pain in those blue eyes, which she was trying so valiantly to disguise with sarcasm. It hurt her that Micah would use her to draw Lopez in. That led him to the question of why it hurt her. And when he saw that answer in her eyes, he could have gone through the floor with shame.

She…loved him. He felt his heart stop and then start again as the thought went through him like electricity. She almost certainly loved him, and she was

doing everything in her power to keep him from seeing it. He remembered her arms around him, her
mouth surrendering to his, her body fluid and soft
under his hands as she yielded instantly to his ardor.
A woman with her past would have a hard time with
lovemaking, yet she'd been willing to let him do anything he liked to her. Why hadn't he questioned that
soft yielding? Why hadn't he known? And she'd
heard what he said to Bojo, feeling that way...

"I swear to you, I won't let Lopez get you," he
said in a firm, sincere tone.

"You mean, you'll try," she replied dully. "I
want a gun, Micah."

"Over my dead body," he said harshly. "You're
not committing suicide."

Her lower lip trembled. She felt trapped. She
looked trapped.

That expression ignited him like fireworks. He
jerked her into his tall, powerful body, and bent to
her mouth before she realized his intent. His warm,
hard mouth bit into her lips with ardent insistence as
his arms enveloped her completely against him. He
felt his body swell instantly, as it always did when
he touched her. He groaned against her mouth and
deepened the kiss, lost in the wonder of being
loved...

Dizzily he registered that she was making a half-
hearted effort to push him away. He felt her cold,
nervous hands on his chest. He lifted his head and
looked at her wary, uncertain little face.

"I won't hurt you," he said softly.

"You're angry," she choked. "It's a punish-
ment..."

"I'm not and it isn't." He bent again, and kissed

her eyelids. His hands worked their way up into the thickness of her hair and then down her back, slowly pressing her to him.

She shivered at the feel of him against her hips.

He chuckled at that telltale sign. "Most men would kill to have such an immediate response to a woman. But I don't suppose you know that."

"You shouldn't…"

He lifted his head again and gave her a look full of amused worldly wisdom. "You think I can will it not to happen, I guess?"

She flushed.

"Sorry, honey, but it doesn't work that way." He moved away just enough to spare her blushes, but his hands slid to her waist and held her in front of him. "I want you to stay in the house," he said, as if he hadn't done anything outrageous at all. "Stay away from windows and porches, too."

She searched his eyes. "If Lopez doesn't see me," she began.

"He knows you're here," he said with faint distaste. "I don't want him to know exactly where you are. I'll have men on every corner of the property and the house for the duration. I won't let you be captured."

She leaned her forehead against him, shivering. "You can't imagine…how it was," she said huskily.

His arms tightened, holding her close. He cursed himself for ever having thought of putting her deliberately in the line of fire. He couldn't imagine he'd been that callous, even briefly. It had been the logical thing to do, and he'd never let emotion get in the way of work. But Callie wasn't like him. She had feelings that were easily bruised, and he'd done a lot of damage already. Those nightmares she had should have convinced him how traumatic her captivity had been, but he hadn't even taken that into consideration when he was setting up Lopez by bringing Callie here.

"I'm sorry," he bit off the words. He wondered if she knew how hard it was to say that.

She blinked away sudden tears. "It's not your fault, you're just trying to save Dad. I love Dad, too, Micah," she said at his chest. "I don't blame you for doing everything you can to keep him safe."

His eyes closed and he groaned silently. "I'm going to do everything I can to keep you safe, too," he told her.

She shrugged. "I know." She pulled away from him with a faint smile to soften the rejection. "Thanks."

He studied her face and realized that he'd never really looked at her so closely before. She had a tiny line of freckles just over her straight little nose. Her light blue eyes had flecks of dark blue in them and she had the faintest little dimple in her cheek when she smiled. He touched her pretty mouth with his fingertips. It was slightly swollen from the hungry, insistent pressure of his lips. She looked rumpled from his ardor, and he liked that, too.

"Take a picture," she said uncomfortably.

"You're pretty," he murmured with an odd smile.

"I'm not, and stop trying to flatter me," she replied, shifting away from him.

"It isn't flattery." He bent and brushed his mouth lightly over her parted lips. She gasped and hung there, her eyes wide and vulnerable on his face when he drew back. Her reaction made him feel taller. He smiled softly. "You don't give an inch, do you? I suppose it's hard for you to trust anyone, after the life you've led."

"I trust Dad," she snapped.

"Yes, but you don't trust me, do you?"

"Not an inch," she agreed, pulling away. "And you don't have to kiss me to make me feel better, either."

"It was to make me feel better," he pointed out, smiling at her surprise. "It did, too."

She shifted her posture a little, confused.

His dark eyes slid over her body, noting the little points that punctuated her breasts and the unsteady breathing she couldn't control. Yes, she wanted him.

She folded her arms over her breasts, curious about why he was staring at them. They felt uncomfortable, but she didn't know why.

"I didn't tell Lisse that you were an embarrassment to me," he said suddenly, and watched her face color.

"It's okay," she replied tersely. "I know I don't have good dress sense. I don't care about clothes most of the time."

"I'm used to women who do, and who enjoy letting men pay for them. The more expensive they are, the better." He sounded jaded and bitter.

She studied his hard face, recognizing disillusionment and reticence. She moved a step closer involuntarily. "You sound...I don't know...cheated, maybe."

"I feel cheated," he said shortly. His eyes were full of harsh memories. "No man likes to think that he's paying for sex."

"Then why do you choose women who want expensive gifts from you?" she asked him bluntly.

His teeth met. "I don't know."

"Don't you, really?" she asked, her eyes soft and curious. "You've always said you don't want to get married, so you pick women who don't want to, either. But that sort of woman only lasts as long as the money does. Or am I wrong?"

He looked down at her from his great height with narrowed eyes and wounded pride. "I suppose you're one of those women who would rush right over to a penniless man and offer to get a second job to help him out of debt!"

She smiled sheepishly, ignoring the sarcasm. "I guess I am." She shrugged. "I scare men off. They don't want me because I'm not interested in what sort of car they drive or the expensive places they can afford to take me to. I like to go walking in the country and pick wildflowers." She peered up at him with a mischievous smile. "The last man I said that to left town two days before he was supposed to. He was doing some accounts for Mr. Kemp and he left skid marks. Mr. Kemp thought it was hilarious. He was a notorious ladies' man, it seems, and he'd actually seduced Mr. Kemp's last secretary."

Micah didn't smile, as she'd expected him to. He looked angry.

She held up a hand. "I don't have designs on you, honest. I know you don't like wildflowers and Lisse is your sort of woman. I'm not interested in you that way, anyhow."

"Considering the way you just kissed me, you might have trouble proving that," he commented dryly.

She cleared her throat. "You kiss very nicely, and I have to get experience where I can."

"Is that it?" he asked dubiously.

She nodded enthusiastically. She swallowed again as the terror of the last hour came back and the eyes she lifted to his were suddenly haunted. "Micah, he's never going to stop, is he?"

"Probably not, unless he has help." He lifted an eyebrow. "I have every intention of helping him, once I've spoken with the authorities."

"What authorities?"

"Never mind. You know nothing. Got it?"

She saluted him. "Yes, sir."

He made a face. "Come on out. We'll have Mac make some sandwiches and coffee. I don't know about you, but I'm hungry."

"I could eat something."

He hesitated before he opened her door. "I really meant what I told you," he said. "Lopez won't get within fifty yards of you as long as there's a breath in my body."

"Thanks," she said unsteadily.

He felt cold inside. He couldn't imagine what had made him tell such lies to Bojo, where she might overhear him. He hadn't meant it, that was honest, but he knew she thought he had. She didn't trust him anymore.

He opened the door to let her go through first. A whiff of the soft rose fragrance she wore drifted up into his nostrils and made his heart jump. She always smelled sweet, and she had a loving nature that was miraculous considering her past. She gave with both hands. He thought of her with Bojo and something snapped inside him.

"Bojo's off limits," he said as she slid past him. "So don't get too attached to him!"

She looked up at him. "What a bunch of sour grapes," she accused, "just because I withdrew my proposal of marriage to you!" She stalked off down the hall.

He opened his mouth to speak, and just laughed instead.

## Chapter Nine

They ate lunch, but conversation among the mercenaries was subdued and Callie got curious glances from all of them. One man, the Mexican called Rodrigo, gave her more scrutiny than the rest. He was a handsome man, tall, slender, dark-haired and dark-eyed, with a grace of movement that reminded her of Micah. But he had a brooding look about him, and he seemed to be always watching her. Once, he smiled, but Micah's appearance sent him away before he could speak to her.

After lunch, Callie asked Bojo about him.

"Rodrigo lost his sister to Lopez's vicious temper," he told her. "She was a nightclub singer who Lopez took a fancy to. He forced himself on her after she rejected Lopez's advances and... She died trying to get away from him. Rodrigo knows what was done to you, and he's angry. You remind him of his sister. She, too, had blue eyes.''

"But he's Latin,'' she began.

"His father was from Denmark,'' he said with a grin. "And blond.''

"Imagine that!''

He gave her a wry glance. "He likes you,'' he said. "But he isn't willing to risk Micah's temper to approach you.''

"You do,'' she said without thinking.

"Ah, but I am indispensable,'' he told her. "Rodrigo is not. He has enemies in many countries overseas and also, Lopez has a contract out on him. This is the only place he has left to go where he has any hope of survival. He wouldn't dare risk alienating Micah.''

She frowned. "I can't think why approaching me would do that. Micah tolerates me, but he still doesn't really like me,'' she pointed out. "I overheard what he said to you, about using me as bait.''

He smiled. "Yes. Curious, is it not, that when one of the other men suggested the same thing, he paid a trip to the dentist?''

"Why?''

"Micah knocked out one of his teeth,'' he confided. "The men agreed that no one would make the suggestion twice.''

She caught her breath. "But I heard him tell you that very thing…!''

"You heard what he wanted me to think,'' he continued. "Micah is jealous of me,'' he added outrageously, and grinned. "You and I are friendly and we have no hostility between us. You don't want anything from me, you see, or from him. He has no idea how to deal with such a woman. He has become used to buying expensive things at a woman's whim, yet you refuse even the gift of a few items of necessary clothing." He shrugged. "It is new for him that neither his good looks nor his wealth make an impression on you. I think he finds that a challenge and it irritates him. He is also very private about his affairs. He doesn't want the men to see how vulnerable he is where you are concerned," he mused. "He had to assign me, along with Peter and Rodrigo, to keep a constant eye on you. He didn't like that. Peter and Rodrigo are no threat, of course, but he is afraid that you are attracted to me." He grinned at her surprise. "I can understand why he thinks this. I hardly need elaborate on my attributes. I am urbane, handsome, sophisticated, generous..." He paused to glance at her wide-eyed, bemused face. "Shall I continue? I should hate to miss acquainting you with any of my virtues."

She realized he was teasing then, and she chuckled. "Okay, go ahead, but I'm not making you any marriage proposals."

His eyebrows arched. "Why not?"

"Micah's put me off men," she said, tongue-in-cheek. "He's already upset because I won't propose to him." She gave him a wicked grin. "Gosh, first Micah, then you! Having this much sex appeal is a curse. Even Lopez is mad to have me!"

He grinned back. She was a unique woman, he thought, and bristling with courage and character. He wondered why Micah didn't see her as he did. The other man was alternately scathing about and protective of Callie, as if his feelings were too ambiguous to unravel. He didn't like Bojo spending time with her, but he kept her carefully at arm's length, even dragging Lisse over for the shopping trip and using her as camouflage. Callie didn't know, but Lisse had been a footnote in Micah's life even in the days when he was attracted to her. She hadn't been around much for almost a year now.

"After we deal with Lopez, you must play down your attractions," he teased. "Providing twenty-four-hour protection is wearing on the nerves."

"You're not kidding," she agreed, wandering farther down the beach. "I'm getting paranoid about dark corners. I always expect someone to be lurking in them." She glanced up at him. "Not rejected suitors," she added wryly.

He clasped his hands behind him and followed along with her, his keen eyes on the horizon, down the beach, up the beach—everywhere. Bojo was certain, as Micah was, that Lopez wasn't likely to give them time to attack him. He was going to storm the island, and soon. They had to be constantly vigilant, if they wanted to live.

"Do you know any self-defense?" Bojo asked her curiously.

"I know a little," she replied. "I took a course in it, but I was overpowered too fast."

"Show me what you know," he said abruptly. "And I will teach you a little more. It never hurts to be prepared.

She did, and he did. She learned enough to protect herself if she had time to use it. She didn't tell him, but she was really scared that Lopez might snatch her out of sight and sound of the mercs. She prayed that she'd have a fighting chance if she was in danger again.

* * *

Callie had convinced herself that an attack would come like a wave, with a lot of men and guns. The last thing she expected was that, when she was lying in her own bed, a man would suddenly appear by the bed and slap a chloroformed handkerchief over her mouth and nose. That was what happened. Outside her patio a waiting small boat on the beach was visible only where she was situated. The dark shadow against the wall managed to bypass every single safeguard of Micah's security system. He slipped into Callie's bedroom with a cloth and a bottle of chloroform and approached the bed where she was asleep.

The first Callie knew of the attack was when she felt a man's hand holding her head steady while a foul-smelling cloth was shoved up under her nose. She came awake at once, but she kept her head, even when she felt herself being carried roughly out of her bedroom onto the stone patio. She knew what to expect this time if she were taken, and she remembered vividly what Bojo had taught her that afternoon. She twisted her head abruptly so that the chloroform missed her face and landed in her hair. Then she got her hands up and slammed them against her captor's ears with all her might.

He cried out in pain and dropped her. She hit the stone-floored patio so hard that she groaned as her hip and leg crashed down onto the flagstones, but she dragged herself to her feet and grabbed at a shovel that the yardman had left leaning against a stone bench close beside her. As her assailant ignored the pain in his fury to pay her back, she swung the shovel and hit him right in the head with it. He made a strange sound and crumpled to the patio. Callie stared out toward the boat, where a dark figure was waiting.

Infuriated by the close call, and feeling very proud of the fact that she'd saved herself this time, she raised the shovel over her head. "Better luck next time, you son of a bitch!" she yelled harshly. "If I had a gun, I'd shoot you!"

Her voice brought Micah and two other men running out onto the patio. They were all armed. The two mercs ran toward the beach, firing as they made a beeline toward the little boat, which had powered up and was sprinting away with incredible speed and very little noise.

Micah stood in front of Callie wearing nothing but a pair of black silk boxer shorts. He had an automatic pistol in one hand. His hair was tousled, as if he'd been asleep. But he was wide-awake now. His face was hard, his dark eyes frightening.

He moved close to her, aware of her body in the thin nylon gown that left her breasts on open display in the light from inside the house. She didn't seem to notice, but he did. He looked at them hungrily before he dragged his gaze back up to her face, fighting a burst of desire as he tried to come to grips with the terror he'd felt when he heard Callie yelling. Thank God she'd had the presence of mind to grab that shovel and knock the man out.

"Are you okay?" he asked curtly.

"I'm better off than he is," she said huskily, swallowing hard. Reaction was beginning to set in now, and her courage was leaking away as the terror of what had almost happened began to tear at her nerves. "He had chloroform. I...I fought free, but...oh, Micah, I was scared to...death!"

She threw herself against him, shuddering in the aftermath of terror. Now that the danger was past, reaction set in with a vengeance. Her arms went under his and around him. Her soft, firm breasts were flattened against his bare stomach because she was so much shorter than he was. Her hands ran over the long, hard muscles of his back, feeling scars there as she pressed closer. He felt the corner of her mouth in the thick hair that covered the hard muscles of his chest. His body reacted predictably to the feel of a near-naked woman and he gasped audibly and stiffened.

Her hips weren't in contact with his, but she felt a tremor run through his powerful body and she pulled back a little, curious, to look up at his strained face. "What's wrong?"

He drew in a steadying breath and moved back. "Nothing! We'll get this guy inside and question him. You don't need to see it," he added firmly. "You should go back into your room..."

"And do what?" she asked, wide-eyed and hurt by his sudden withdrawal. "You think I can go to sleep now?"

"Stupid assumption," he murmured, moving restively as his body tormented him. "I can call Lisse and let her stay with you."

"No!" She lifted her chin with as much pride as she had left. "I'll get dressed. Bojo will sit up with me if I ask him..."

"The hell he will!" he exploded, his eyes glittering.

She took a step backward. He was frightening

when he looked like that. He seemed more like the stranger he'd once been than the man who'd been so kind to her in past days.

"I'll get dressed and you can stay with me tonight," he snapped. "Obviously it's asking too much to expect you to stay by yourself!" That was unfair, he realized at once, and he ground his teeth. He couldn't help it. He was afraid to be in the same room with her in the dark, but not for the reason she thought.

She took another step backward, pride reasserting itself. Her chin came up. "No, thanks!" she said. "If you'll just get me a gun and load it and show me how to shoot it, I won't have any problem with being alone."

She sounded subdued, edgy, still frightened despite that haughty look she was giving him. He was overreacting. It infuriated him that she'd had to rescue herself. It infuriated him that he wanted her. He was jealous of his men, angry that she was vulnerable, and fighting with all his might to keep from giving in to his desire for her. She was a marrying woman. She was a virgin. It was hopeless.

Worst of all, she'd almost been kidnapped again and on his watch. He'd fallen asleep, worn-out by days of wear and tear and frustrated desire. Lopez had almost had her tonight. He blamed himself for not taking more precautions, for putting her in harm's way. He should have protected her. He should have realized that Lopez was desperate enough to try anything, including an assault on the house itself. So much for his security net. Upgrades were very definitely needed. But right now, she needed comfort, and he wasn't giving it to her.

He glanced toward the beach. Out beyond it, the little boat had stilled in the water and seemed to be sinking. A dark figure struck out toward the shore.

"Peter, get him!" Micah yelled.

The young man gave him a thumbs-up signal. The tall young man tossed down his weapon, jerked off his boots and overclothes and dived into the water. The assailant tried to get away, but Peter got him. There was a struggle and seconds later, Peter dragged the man out of the water and stood over him where he lay prone on the beach.

Rodrigo came running back up from the beach just about the time the man who'd tried to carry Callie off woke up and rubbed his aching head.

"I told Peter to take the other man around the side of the house to the boat shed."

"Good work," Micah said.

"Oh, look, he's all right," Callie murmured, her eyes narrowed on the downed man who was beginning to move and groan. "What a shame!"

Micah glanced at her. "Bloodthirsty girl," he chided, and grinned despite his churning emotions.

"Well, he tried to kidnap me," she bit off, finally getting her nerve and her temper back. She remembered the chloroform and her eyes blazed. "All I had to hand was a lousy shovel, that's why he's all right."

He turned to the other man. "Rodrigo, get this guy around to the boat shed to keep Peter's captive company. Strip them both, tie them up and gag them. I've got to make a few preparations and I'll be along to question them. Do *not* tell Bojo anything, except that the police have been notified. You can phone them to pick up Lopez's henchmen an hour from now, no sooner.''

''I know what you're thinking. It won't work,'' Rodrigo said, trying to reason with him. ''Lopez will be expecting his men back, if he hasn't already seen what happened.''

''Have you got the infrareds on you?''

Rodrigo nodded and pulled out what looked like a fancy pair of binoculars.

''Check the area off the beach for Lopez's yacht.''

''It's clear for miles right now. No heat signatures.''

''Heat signatures?'' Callie murmured.

''We have heat-seeking technology,'' Micah explained. ''We can look right into a house or a room in the dark and see everything alive in it, right through the walls.''

''You're kidding!'' she exclaimed.

''He's not,'' Rodrigo said, his dark eyes narrowing as he noted the gown and the pretty form underneath.

Micah knew what the other man was seeing, and it angered him. He stepped in front of Callie, and the action was blatant enough to get Rodrigo moving.

''Where do you think Lopez's yacht is?'' Callie asked.

''It'll be somewhere close around. Let's just hope the man Peter caught was too rattled to call Lopez while he was being shot at. I'm sure he had a cell phone. Get out my diving gear and some C-4. And don't say a word to Bojo. Got that? It will work.''

''What will work?'' Callie asked.

''Never mind,'' Micah said. ''Thanks, Rodrigo. I'm going to get Callie back inside.''

"I'll deal with our guest," Rodrigo said, and turned at once to his chore.

Micah drew Callie along with him, from the patio to the sliding glass doors her assailant had forced, and down the hall to her bedroom. On the way, he noticed that two other doors had been opened, as if her captor had looked in them in search of her. His bedroom was closer to the front of the house.

He drew her inside her room and closed the door behind them, pausing to lay the automatic on a table nearby. "Did he hurt you?" he asked at once.

"He dropped me on the patio. I bruised my hip...Micah, no!" she exclaimed, pushing at the big, lean hand that was pulling up her nylon gown.

"I've seen more of you than this," he reminded her.

"But..."

He swept her up in his arms and carried her to the bed, easing her down gently onto the sheet where the covers had been thrown back by her captor. He sat down beside her and pulled up the gown, smiling gently at the pale pink cotton briefs she was wearing.

"Just what I'd expect," he murmured. "Functional, not sexy."

"Nobody sees my underthings except me," she bit off. "Will you stop?"

He pushed the gown up to her waist, ignoring her protests, and winced when he saw her upper thigh and hip. "You're going to have a whopper of a bruise on your leg," he murmured, drawing down the elastic of the briefs. "Your hip didn't fare much better."

His thumb was against the soft, warm skin of her lower stomach and the other one was poised beside her head on the pillow while he looked at her bruises. She didn't think he was doing it on purpose, but that thumb seemed to be moving back and forth in a very arousing way. Her body liked it. She moved restlessly on the sheet, shivering a little with unexpected pleasure.

"A few bruises are...are better than being kidnapped," she whispered shakily. Her wide eyes met his. "I was so scared, Micah!"

His hand spread on her hip. His narrow black eyes met hers. "So was I, when I heard you shouting," he said huskily. "He almost had you!"

"Almost," she agreed, her breath jerking out. "I'm still shaking."

His fingers contracted. "I'm going to give you a sedative," he said, rising abruptly. "You need to sleep. You never will, in this condition."

He left her there and went to get his medical kit. He was back almost at once. He opened the bag and drew out a small vial of liquid and a prepackaged hypodermic syringe. This would alleviate her fear of being alone tonight and give him time to get his rampaging hormones under control.

She watched him fill the syringe effortlessly. It was a reminder that he'd studied medicine.

"Have you ever thought of going back to finish your residency?" she asked him.

He shook his head. "Too tame." He smiled in her general direction as he finished filling the syringe. "I don't think I could live without adrenaline rushes."

"Doctors have those, too," she pointed out, watching him extend her arm and tap a vein in the curve of her elbow. "You're going to put it in there?" she asked worriedly.

"It's quicker. You won't get addicted to this," he added, because she looked apprehensive. "Close your eyes. I'll try not to hurt you."

She did close her eyes, but she felt the tiny prick of the needle and winced. But it was over quickly and he was dabbing her arm with alcohol on a cotton ball.

"It won't knock you out completely," he said when he'd replaced everything in the kit. "But it will relax you."

She blinked. She felt *very* relaxed. She peered up at him with wide, soft eyes. "I wish you liked me," she said.

His eyebrows levered up. "I do."

"Not really. You don't want me around. I'm not pretty like her."

"Her?"

"Lisse." She sighed and stretched lazily, one leg rising so that the gown fell away from her pretty leg, leaving it bare. "She's really beautiful, and she has nice, big breasts. Mine are just tiny, and I'm so ordinary. Gosh, I'd love to have long blond hair and big breasts."

He glanced at the bag and back at her. "This stuff works on you like truth serum, doesn't it?" he murmured huskily.

She sat up with a misty smile and shrugged the gown off, so that it fell to her waist. Her breasts had hard little tips that aroused him the instant he saw them. "See?" she asked. "They look like acorns. Hers look like cantaloupes."

He couldn't help himself. He stared at her breasts helplessly, while his body began to swell with an urgency that made him shiver. He was vulnerable tonight.

"Yours are beautiful," he said softly, his eyes helplessly tracing them.

"No, they're not. You don't even like feeling them against you. You went all stiff and pushed me away, out on the patio. It's been like that since…Micah, what are you…doing?" she gasped as his hungry mouth abruptly settled right on top of a hard nipple and began to suckle it. "Oh…glory!" she cried out, arching toward him with a lack of restraint that was even more arousing. Her nails bit into his scalp through his thick hair, coaxing him even closer. "I like that. I…really like that!" she whispered frantically. "I like it, I like it, I…!"

"I should be shot for this," he uttered as he suckled her. "But I want you. Oh God, I want you so!" His teeth opened and nipped her helplessly.

She drew back suddenly, apprehensively as she felt his teeth, her eyes questioning.

He could barely breathe, and he knew there was no way on earth he was going to be able to stop. It was already too late. Danger was an aphrodisiac. "You don't like my teeth on you," he whispered. "All right. It's all right. We'll try this."

His fingers traced around her pert breast gently and he bent to take her mouth tenderly under his lips. She had no willpower. She opened her lips for him and clung as he eased her down onto the cool sheets.

"Don't let me do this, Callie," he ground out in a last grab at sanity, even as he shed his boxer shorts. "Tell me to stop!"

"I couldn't, not if it meant my life," she murmured, her body on fire for him. Her mind wasn't even working. She held on for dear life and pulled his mouth down harder on hers. She was shivering with pleasure. "I want you to do it," she whispered brazenly. "I want to feel you naked in my arms. I want to make love…!"

"Callie. Sweet baby!" he whispered hoarsely as he felt her hands searching down his flat belly to the source of his anguish. She touched him and he was lost, totally lost. He pressed her hard into the mattress while his mouth devoured hers. It was too late to pull back, too late to reason with her. She was drugged and uninhibited, and her hands were touching him in a way that pushed him right over the edge.

Callie lifted against him, aware of his nudity and the delight of touching him where she'd never have dreamed of touching him if she hadn't been drugged. But she'd always wanted to touch him like that, and it felt wonderful. Her body moved restlessly with little darts of pleasure as he began to discover her, too.

She enjoyed the feel of his body, the touch of his hands. Her skin felt very hot, and when she realized that the gown and her underwear were gone, it didn't matter, because she felt much more comfortable. Then he started touching her in a way she'd never been touched. She gasped. Her body tensed, but she moved toward his hand, burying her face in his neck as the delicious sensations made her pulse with delight. His skin was damp and very hot. She could hear the rasp of his breathing, she could feel it in her hair as he began to caress her very intimately.

Of course, it was wrong to let him do something so outrageous, but it felt too good to stop. She kept coaxing him with sharp little movements of her hips until he was touching her where her body wanted him to. Now the pleasure was stark and urgent. She opened her legs. Her nails bit into his nape and she clung fiercely.

"It's all right," he whispered huskily. "I won't stop. I'll be good to you."

She clung closer. Her body shivered. She was suddenly open to his insistent exploration and with embarrassment she felt herself becoming very damp where his fingers were. She stiffened.

"It's natural," he breathed into her ear. "Your body is supposed to do this."

"It is?" She couldn't look at him. "It isn't repulsive to you?"

"It's the most exciting thing I've ever felt," he whispered. His powerful body shifted so that he was lying directly over her, his hair-roughened legs lazily brushing against hers while he teased her mouth with his lips and her body with his fingers.

Her arms were curled around his neck and the sensations were so sweet that she began to gasp rhythmically. Her hips were lifting and falling with that same rhythm as she fed on the delicious little jabs of pleasure that accompanied every sensual movement.

He began to shudder, too. It was almost as if he weren't in control of himself. But that was ridiculous. Micah was always in control.

His teeth tugged at her upper lip and then at her lower one, his tongue sliding sinuously inside her mouth in slow, teasing thrusts. She felt her breasts going very tight. He was lying against her in an unexpectedly intimate way. She felt body hair against her breasts and her belly. Then she felt him there, *there,* in a contact that she'd never dreamed of sharing with him.

Despite her languor, her eyes opened and looked straight into his. She could actually see the desire that was riding him, there in his taut face and glittering eyes and flattened lips. He was shivering. She liked seeing him that way. She smiled lazily and deliberately brushed her body up against him. He groaned.

Slowly he lifted himself just a little. "Look down," he whispered huskily. "Look at me. I want you to see how aroused I am for you."

Her eyes traced the path of thick, curling blond-tipped hair from the wedge on his muscular chest, down his flat belly, and to another wedge…heavens! He had nothing on. And more than that, he was…he was…

Her misty gaze shot back up to meet his. She should be protesting. He was so aroused that a maiden lady with silver hair couldn't have mistaken it. She felt suddenly very small and vulnerable, almost fragile. But he wanted her, and she wanted him so badly that she couldn't find a single word of protest. Even if he never touched her again, she'd have this one time to live on for the rest of her miserable, lonely life. She'd be his lover, if only this once. Nothing else mattered. Nothing!

Her body lifted to brush helplessly against his while she looked at him. She was afraid. She was excited. She was on fire. She was wanton…

His hand went between their hips and began to invade her body, where it was most sensitive. Despite the pleasure that ensued, she felt a tiny stab of discomfort.

"I can feel it," he whispered, his eyes darkening as his body went taut. "It's wispy, like a spiderweb.'' He shifted sensuously. His body began to invade hers in a slow, teasing motion, and he watched her the whole time. ''Are you going to let me break it, Callie?'' he whispered softly.

''Break…it?''

''Your maidenhead. I want it.'' He moved his hips down and his whole face clenched as he felt the veil of her innocence begin to separate. His hands clenched beside her head on the pillow and the eyes that looked down into hers were tortured. His whole body shuddered with each slow movement of his hips. ''I want…you! Callie!'' he groaned hoarsely, his eyes closing. ''Callie …baby…let me have you,'' he whispered jerkily. ''Let me have…all of you! Let me teach you pleasure…''

He seemed to be in pain. She couldn't bear that. She slid her calves slowly over his and gasped when she felt his body tenderly penetrating hers with the action, bringing a tiny wave of pleasure. She gasped again.

He arched above her, groaning. His eyes held hers as he moved slowly, carefully. He watched her wince and he hesitated. He moved again, and she bit her lip. He moved one more time, and she tensed and then suddenly relaxed, so unexpectedly that his possession of her was complete in one involuntary movement.

It was incredible, he thought, his body as taut as steel as he looked down into her wide, curious eyes with awe as he became her lover. He could feel her, like a warm silk glove. She was a virgin. He was having her. She was giving herself. He moved experimentally, and her lips parted on a helpless breath.

His lean hands slid under her dark hair and cradled

her head while he began to move on her. One of his thighs pushed at hers, nudging it further away from the throbbing center of her body. The motion lifted her against him in a blind grasp at pleasure.

"I never thought...it would be you," she whispered feverishly.

"I never thought it would be anyone else," he replied, his eyes hot and narrow and unblinking. "I watched you when I went completely into you," he whispered and smiled when she gasped. "Now, you can watch me," he murmured roughly. "Watch me. I'll let you see...everything I feel!"

She shivered as his hips began to move sinuously, more insistently, increasing the pleasure.

He caught one of her hands and drew it between them, coaxing it back to his body. He groaned at the contact and guided her fingers to the heart of him.

She let him teach her. It was so sweet, to lie naked in his arms, and watch him make love to her. He was incredibly tender. He gave her all the time in the world before he became insistent, before his kisses devoured, before his hand pinned her hips and his whole body became an instrument of the most delicious torture. He looked down at her with blazing dark eyes, his face clenched in passion, his body shivering with urgency as he poised over her.

"Don't close your eyes," he groaned when stars were exploding in his head. "I want to see them...the very second...that you go over the edge under me!"

The words were as arousing as the sharp, violent motion of his hips as he began to drive into her. She thought he became even more potent as the tempo and the urgency increased. He held her eyes until she became blind with the first stirrings of ecstasy and her sharp, helpless cry of surprised pleasure was covered relentlessly by his mouth.

She writhed under him, sobbing with the sensation of fulfillment, her body riveted to his as convulsions made her ripple like a stormy wave. She clutched his upper arms, her nails biting in, as the ripples became almost painful in their delight. Seconds later, she felt him climax above her. His harsh, shuddering groan was as alien a sound as her own had been seconds before. She wrapped her arms around him and held on for dear life, cuddling him, cradling him, as he endured the mindless riptide and finally, finally, went limp and heavy in her arms with a whispery sigh.

"You looked at me...when it happened," she whispered with wonder. "And I saw you, I watched you." She shivered, holding him tight. Her body rippled with the tiny movement, and she laughed secretly and moaned as she felt the pleasure shoot through her. "Do it again," she pleaded. "Make me scream this time...!"

He was still shivering. "Oh, God, ...no!" he bit off. "Be still!" He held her down, hard, drawing in a sharp breath as he fought the temptation to do what she asked. He closed his eyes and his teeth clenched as he jerked back from her abruptly.

She gasped as his weight receded. There was a slight discomfort, and then he was on his feet beside the bed, grabbing up his boxer shorts with a furious hand.

She stared at him with diminishing awareness. She was deliciously relaxed. She felt great. Why was he cursing like that. She blinked vacantly. "You're very angry. What's wrong?"

''What's wrong!'' He turned to look down at her. She was sprawled nude in glorious abandon, looking so erotic that he almost went to his knees with the arousal that returned with a vengeance.

She smiled lazily and yawned. ''Gosh, that was good. So good!'' Her eyelids felt very heavy. She sprawled even more comfortably. ''Even better than the last time.''

''What last time?'' he demanded, outraged.

She yawned again. ''That other dream,'' she mumbled, rolling onto her side. ''So many dreams. So embarrassing. So erotic! But this was the best dream, though. The very…best…''

Her voice trailed away and he realized all at once that she'd fallen asleep. She didn't understand what had happened. She'd been full of sedative and she'd let him seduce her, thinking she was just dreaming. She thought the whole thing was nothing more than another dream. No wonder she hadn't protested!

''God in heaven, what have I done!'' he asked her oblivious form. There was a smear of blood on the white sheet.

Micah ground his teeth together and damned his lack of control. He hadn't had a woman in a very long time, and he'd wanted Callie since the day he'd met her. But that was no excuse for taking advantage of her while she was under the influence of a sedative. Even if she had come on to him with the most incredibly erotic suggestions. He'd seduced her and that was that.

He went to the bathroom, wet a washcloth and bathed her body as gently as he could. She was sleeping so soundly that she never noticed a thing. He put her briefs and gown back on her and put her under the sheet. He'd have to hope she didn't notice the stain, or, if she did, assumed it was an old one.

He dressed, hating himself, and went out of the room after checking the security net. He still had to go after Lopez, and now his mind was going to be full of Callie sobbing with pleasure under the crush of his body. And what if there were consequences?

## Chapter Ten

With a face as grim as death, Micah pulled on his black wet suit and fins and checked the air in his tanks and the mouthpiece and face mask. He sheathed the big knife he always carried on covert missions. To the belt around his waist, he attached a waterproof carry pack. He'd interrogated one of the men, who'd been far too intimidated not to tell him what he wanted to know about Lopez's setup on the yacht, the number and placement of his men and his firepower.

"I should go with you," Rodrigo told him firmly.

"You can't dive," Micah said. "Besides, this is a one-man job. If I don't make it, it will be up to you and Bojo to finish it. But whatever happens," he added curtly, and with a threatening stare, "don't let them get Callie."

"I won't. I swear it," Rodrigo said heavily.

"Tell Bojo where I've gone after I've gone, but only after I'm gone," he added. "Don't let him follow me." He picked up a small device packed with plastique and shoved it into the waterproof bag on his belt and sealed it.

"Once you set the trigger, you'll only have a few minutes to get free of the ship. If the engines fire up while you're placing the bomb, you'll be chum," Rodrigo said worriedly. "You already look exhausted. Even if everything goes right, how will you make that swim and turn around and come back in time?"

"If I can't get free in that amount of time, I'm in the wrong business," he told Rodrigo. "I'd disgrace my expensive government training. How many men on the yacht right now?"

Rodrigo nodded toward the yacht, which had just come into view in the past ten minutes. It was out very far, almost undetectable without exotic surveillance devices. But they had a device that used a heat sensor with a telescopic lens, and they could see inside the ship. "The crew, Lopez, and six henchmen. It's suicide to do this alone."

"I'm not letting him try again," he said shortly, and his eyes were blazing. "I've put Callie's life at risk already, because I was arrogant enough to think she was safe here. She could have been killed tonight while I was asleep in my bed. I won't get over that in a hurry. I'm not going to give her to Lopez, no matter what it costs me." He put a hand on Rodrigo's shoulder. "Listen to me. If anything goes wrong, you tell Bojo that I want him to take care of her from now on. There's enough money in my Swiss account to support her and my father for life, in any style they like. You tell Bojo I said to see that she gets it, less the sum we agreed on for all of you. Promise me!''

"Of course I promise." Rodrigo's eyes narrowed. "You look…different."

*I've just seduced a virgin who thinks she was having an erotic dream,* he thought with black humor. *No wonder I look different.* "It's been a long night," he said. "Call the police an hour from now." He looked at his expensive commando watch, the one with a tiny sharp knife blade that could be released from the edge of the face with a light touch. "Coming up on fourteen hundred and ten hours…almost… almost…hack!''

Rodrigo had set his watch to the same time. He gave Micah a long, worried look as the taller man put on his face mask and adjusted the mouthpiece.

*"Dios te protégé,"* Rodrigo said gently. God protect you.

Micah smiled and put the mouthpiece in. Seconds later, he was in the water, under the water, headed out toward the yacht. It was a distance of almost half a mile, and Rodrigo was uneasy. But Micah had been a champion swimmer in his school days, and he held some sort of record for being able to hold his breath underwater. He looked very tired, though, and that was going to go against him. Odd, Rodrigo thought, that a man who'd just gotten out of bed should look exhausted. And after the culprits had been dealt with so quickly and effectively, which couldn't have tired him. He hoped Micah would succeed. He checked his watch, glanced at the bound and gagged captives in their underwear, and shrugged.

"How sad for you, *compadres,* that your futures will be seen through vertical bars. But, then, your choice of employer leaves so much to be desired!''

He turned away, recalling that Micah had told him to phone the police an hour after he'd gone. But he hesitated to do that, orders or not. Timing was going to be everything here. If there was a holdup planting the charge, and if Lopez had someone on the payroll in Nassau, the show was over. Lopez would get word of the failed kidnapping attempt in time to blow Micah out of the water. Micah couldn't have been thinking straight. Rodrigo would do that for him. He would watch Micah's back. Now he prayed that his boss could complete this mission without discovery. If ever a man deserved his fate, it was Manuel Lopez. He gave Mexicans a bad name, and for that alone Rodrigo was anxious to see him go down.

It took Micah a long time to reach the boat. He was exhausted from the mindless pleasure Callie had given him. Making love with her just before the most dangerous mission of recent years had to be evidence of insanity. But it had been so beautiful, so tender. He could still hear her soft, surprised cries of pleasure. The memory was the sort a man wouldn't mind going down into the darkness for. Of course, it wasn't helping him focus on the task at hand. He forcibly put the interlude to the back of his mind and swam on.

He paused as he reached the huge yacht, carefully working his way toward the huge propellers at the stern, which were off right now but would start again eventually. If they started while he was near them, he'd be caught in their turbulent wake and dragged right into those cruel blades to be dismembered before he set the charge. *Not* the end he hoped for.

He kept himself in place with slow movements of his fins while he shone an underwater light hooked to his belt on the bomb package enclosed in the waterproof bag. He drew it out, very carefully, and secured it to a metallic connection behind the propellers. It stuck like glue. He positioned the light so that he could work with his hands while he wired the charge into the propeller system. It was meticulous work, and he was really tired. But he finally secured the connection and double-checked the explosive package. Yes. The minute the turbine engines fired, the ship would blow up.

The problem was, he was almost too tired to swim back. He was going to have to give himself thirty minutes to get back to the shore, and pray that Lopez didn't have his men fire up those propellers until he was out of harm's way.

He gave the ship's hull a gentle pat, with a momentary twinge of regret at having to destroy such a beautiful yacht. Then he turned and moved slowly, cautiously, around toward the bow of the ship. There was a ladder hanging down from the side. He passed it with idle curiosity and held onto it while he floated, letting his body relax and rest. He just happened to look up while he was hanging from it.

Just above the surface, a man was aiming an automatic weapon down at him through the water.

He couldn't get away. He was too tired. Besides, the man wasn't likely to miss at this range. Salute the flag and move on, he mused philosophically. Nobody lived forever, and his death would serve a noble cause. All he had to do was make them think he'd come aboard to use the knife on Lopez, so they wouldn't start looking for bombs. They had enough time to find and disarm it if he didn't divert them. The waterproof bag on his hip was going to be hard to explain. So was his flashlight. Fortunately the light

fit into the bag and weighed it down. He unhooked
the bag and closed it out of sight while the man
above motioned angrily for him to come up the ladder. He let the bag drop and it sank even as he started
the climb to his own death. He might get a chance
at Lopez before they killed him, because Lopez
would want to gloat.

He padded onto the deck in his breathing equipment and fins, which the man ordered him in Spanish
to take off.

Micah tossed his gear aside, carefully, because the
man with the gun was nervous. If he had any chance
at all to escape, he could make the distance without
his equipment if he swam—assuming he wasn't shot
to death in the process. He had to hope for a break,
but it wasn't likely. This was the situation that every
working mercenary had to consider when he chose
the lifestyle. Death could come at any moment, unexpectedly.

He stood glaring down at the smaller man. Even
with his automatic weapon, the drug lord's man
didn't seem too confident. He backed up two more
steps. Micah noted the hasty retreat and tensed to
make his move. But only seconds later, Lopez and
two more men—armed men—came up on deck.

Lopez stared at Micah for a minute and then rec-
ognition flashed in his dark eyes. "Micah Steele, I
presume," he drawled in accented English. He put
his hands behind him and walked around Micah like
an emperor inspecting a new slave. "You lack pro-
ficiency, don't you? Were you planning to use this
on me while I slept?" he added, jerking the big
bowie knife out of its sheath. "A nasty weapon. Very
nasty." He put the point against Micah's wet suit
just below the nipple. "A hard thrust, and you cease

to exist. You were careless. Now you will pay the price for it.'' His face hardened. ''Where are my two men that I sent to reclaim your stepsister?''

Micah smiled calmly. ''The police have them by now. I expect they'll spill their guts trying to save themselves.''

''They would not dare,'' Lopez said easily. ''They fear me.''

''They won't fear you if you're in prison,'' he replied easily. ''Or dead.''

Lopez laughed. It amused him that this mercenary wasn't begging for his life. He was used to men who did.

''Your attempt at diversion serves no purpose. We both know that my men are on the way back with their captive even now. In fact,'' he added with a deliberate smile, ''I had a phone call just before you were discovered, telling me that she was safely bound and gagged. Your men are too numerous for them to fight, so they are hiding her some distance from your house until the coast is clear and they can get here with the boat.'' He chuckled maliciously.

Micah surmised that a cell phone had been discovered on one of the men, and Rodrigo had used it to reassure Lopez. A stroke of genius, and it might have worked, if Micah hadn't been careless and let himself get captured like a raw recruit.

''I am fond of knives,'' Lopez murmured, and ran his fingers over the carved bone handle almost like a caress. He looked at Micah as he traced the pattern in it. ''This time, I will not give your stepsister to my men. I will use the knife on her myself.'' His eyes were cold, hard, unfeeling. ''I will skin her alive,'' he said softly. ''And with every strip that comes off, I will remind her that you were careless enough to let her be apprehended a second time." His eyes blazed. "You invaded my home to take her from me. No one humiliates me in such a manner and lives to gloat about it. You will die and your sister will die, and in such a way that it will frighten anyone who sees it."

Micah studied the little man with contempt, seeing the years of death and torture that had benefited Lopez. The drug lord could buy people, yachts, countries. He had enormous power. But it was power built on a foundation of greed, floored with blood and tears. If ever a man deserved to go down, it was Lopez.

"You are very quiet, Micah Steele," Lopez said suddenly, and his eyes narrowed suspiciously.

"I was thinking that I've never encountered anyone as evil as you, Lopez," he said quietly. "You have no conscience at all."

Lopez shrugged. "I am what I am," he said simply. "In order to accumulate great wealth, one has to be willing to take great risks. I have been poor. I never want to be poor again."

"Plenty of people prefer it to murder."

Lopez only laughed. "You are, how is it said, stalling for time," he said abruptly. "Are you hoping to be rescued? Or are you hoping that perhaps one of your men has checked on your stepsister and found her missing from her room? That is not likely. My men are quite expert. Playing for time will avail you nothing."

Micah could have told him that he was using the time to rest from his exhaustive swim, marshaling his strength for an all-out assault. If they took him down, he vowed, he was at least going to take Lopez with him, even if he died with the drug lord's neck in his hands.

"Or you might think it possible to overpower all of us and escape." He laughed again. "I think that I will wait to begin your interrogation until your stepsister is on board with us. Carlos!" he called to a henchman. "Tell the captain to start the engines and move us a little closer to the island."

Micah's heart stopped dead, but not a trace of fear or apprehension showed on his face. Lopez was watching him very closely, as if he suspected something. Micah simply smiled, considering that it was the fortunes of war that sometimes you didn't win. At least Callie was safe. He hadn't lost completely as long as she survived. He took a relaxing breath and waited for the explosion.

Lopez's henchman was almost up the steps to the pilothouse when Lopez wheeled suddenly.

"Wait!" Lopez called his man back suddenly and Micah fought to keep from showing his relief. "I do not trust you, Steele," Lopez added. "I think perhaps you want me to go closer to your island, to give your men a shot at us, here on the deck. If so, you are going to be disappointed." He turned to the man, Carlos. "Take him below and tie him up. Then I want you and Juan to take one of the boats and follow in the steps of Ramon and Jorge. They must be somewhere near the house waiting for the mercenaries to give up the search or locate it elsewhere. You can help them bring the girl back."

*"Si, señor,"* Carlos said at once, and stuck the automatic weapon in Micah's back. "You will go ahead of me, *señor,*" he told Micah. "And remember, there will be an armed man at the foot of the steps. Escape is not possible. *¡Vaya!*"

Micah gave Lopez one last contemptuous look before he went down the steps into the bowels of the ship. So far, so good. They were convinced that their men on shore were safe and had Callie. They weren't going to start the ship just yet, thank God. He had one last chance to absolve himself. He was going to take it, regardless of the price.

The henchman tied him up in a chair with nylon cord at his wrists and ankles. The cord was tight enough to cut off the circulation. Micah felt his hands and feet going numb, but he wasn't going to protest.

"What a nice fish we caught," Lopez's man chuckled. "And soon, big fish, we will fillet you and your stepsister together." His eyes narrowed and he smiled coldly. "You have embarrassed my boss. No one is allowed to do that. You must be made an example of. I would not wish to be in your shoes." He looked pointedly at Micah's bare feet. "Hypothetically speaking," he added. "Enjoy your last minutes of life, *señor*."

The small man left Micah in the stateroom, which was obviously some sort of guest room. There was a bed and a dresser and this chair in it, and it was very small. One of the officers of the ship might sleep here, he reasoned.

Now that he was alone—and he wouldn't be for long—he might have just enough time to free himself. Micah touched the button on his watch that extended the small but very sharp little knife blade concealed in the watch face. He cut himself free with very little effort. But the most dangerous part was yet to come. There were men everywhere, all armed. The one thing he had going for him was that it was dark and Lopez had very few lights on deck at the moment, hoping not to be noticed by Micah's men.

He eased out into the corridor and listened. He heard a man's voice humming a Mexican drinking song off-key nearby. Watching up and down the hall with every step, he eased into the galley. A man just a little smaller than he was stirring something in a very big stainless-steel pot. He was wearing black slacks and a black sweater with an apron over them. Micah smiled.

He caught the man from behind and stunned him. Carefully he eased the cook back behind the stove and began to strip him. He pulled off his scuba gear and donned the cook's outerwear, taking time to dress the cook in his own diving suit. The cook had dark hair, but it wouldn't matter. All he had to do was look like Micah at a distance.

He got the cook over his shoulder and made his way carefully to the ladder that led up onto the deck. Lopez was talking to two other men, and not looking in Micah's direction. What supreme self-confidence, Micah thought. Pity to spoil it.

He slapped the cook and brought him around. In the next instant, he threw the man overboard on the side that faced away from Micah's island.

*"¡Steele ha escapado!"* Micah yelled in Spanish. *"¡Se fue alla, a la izquierda, en el Mar!"* Steele has escaped, he went there, to the left, in the sea!

There was a cry of fury from Lopez, followed by harsh orders, and the sound of running feet. Micah followed the other men, managing to blend in, veering suddenly to the other side of the ship.

Just as he got there, he was faced with a henchman who hadn't followed the others. The man had an automatic weapon in his hands and he was hesitating, his eyes trying to see Micah, who was half in shadow so that his blond hair didn't give the game away. If the man pulled that trigger...

*"Es que usted esta esperando una cerveza?"* he shot at the man angrily. *"¡Vaya! ¡Steele esta alla!"* What are you waiting for, a beer? Get going, Steele's over there!

He hesitated with his heart in his throat, waiting, waiting...

All at once, there was a shout from the other side of the ship. The man who was holding Micah at bay still hesitated, but the noise got louder.

*"¡Vaya!"* he repeated. He waved the man on urgently with a mumbled Spanish imprecation about Steele and his useless escape attempt. In that space of seconds before they discovered the man in the water was not Micah, their escaping captive got over the rail and into the ocean and struck out back toward the shore. He kept his strokes even and quick, and he zigzagged. Even if Lopez's men spotted him, they were going to have to work at hitting him from that distance. Every few yards, he submerged and swam underwater. Any minute now, he told himself, and thanked God he'd had just enough rest to allow him a chance of making it to shore before he was discovered and killed.

He heard loud voices and a searchlight began sweeping the water. Micah dived under again and held his breath. With a little bit of luck, they might pass right over him, in his black clothing. He blended in very well with the ocean.

There was gunfire. He ground his teeth together and prayed they'd miss him. Probably they were shooting blind, hoping to hit him with a lucky shot.

Odd, though, the gunfire sounded closer than that...

He came up for air, to snatch a breath, and almost collided with his own swift motorboat, with Bojo driving it and firing an automatic rifle toward Lopez and his men at the same time.

"Climb in, boss!" Bojo called, and kept shooting.

"Remind me to give you a raise," Micah panted as he dragged himself over the side and into the rocking boat. "Good work. Good work! Now get the hell out of here before they blow us out of the water!"

Bojo swung the boat around masterfully and imitated the same zigzag pattern that Micah had used when he swam.

"Lopez is mad now," Micah said with a glittery smile. "If there's any justice left in the world, he'll try to move in closer to get a better shot at us."

"We hope," Bojo said solemnly, still dodging bullets.

Micah looked back toward the ship, now clearly visible against the horizon. He thought of all Lopez's helpless victims, of whole families in tiny little Mexican towns who had been mowed down with automatic weapons for daring to help the authorities catch the local pushers. He thought of the hard fight to shut down Lopez's distribution network slated for operation in Jacobsville, Texas. He thought of Callie in that murderous assassin's hands, of the knife cut on her pretty little breast where the point had gone in. He thought of Callie dead, tortured, an anguished expression locked forever into those gentle features. He thought of his father, who would have been Lopez's next target. He thought of Lisa Monroe Parks's young husband in the DEA who'd been killed on Lopez's orders. He thought of all the law enforcement people who'd risked their lives and the lives of their families to stop Lopez.

"It's retribution time, Lopez," Micah said absently, watching the big ship with somber eyes. "Life calls in the bets for us all, sooner or later. But you're overdue, you drug-dealing son of a...!"

Before the last word left his lips, there was a huge fireburst where the ship had been sitting in the water. Flames rolled up and up and up, billowing black smoke into the atmosphere. The sound rocked the boat, and pieces of the yacht began falling from the sky in a wide circumference. Micah and Bojo ducked down in the boat and covered their heads as Bojo increased their speed and changed direction, hoping to miss the heavier metal parts that were raining down with wood and fabric.

They made it to the boat dock and jumped out as the last pieces of what had been Lopez's yacht fell into the water.

Mercenaries came rushing down from the house, all armed, to see what had happened.

"Say goodbye to Lopez," Micah told them, eyes narrowed with cold scrutiny.

They all watched the hull of the ship, still partially intact, start to sink. To their credit, none of them cheered or laughed or made a joke. Human lives had been lost. It was no cause for celebration, not even when the ringleader was as bad as Lopez. It had been necessary to eliminate him. He was crazed with vengeance and dangerous to the world at large.

Rodrigo came up beside them. "Glad to see you still alive, boss," he said.

Micah nodded. "It was close. I was too tired to swim back. He caught me at the ladder like a raw recruit."

There was a faint sound from Peter, the newest of

the group. "I thought slips were my signature," he told Micah.

"Even veterans can step the wrong way and die for it," Micah told him gently. "That's why you always do it by the book and make sure you've got backup. I broke all the rules, but I didn't want to put anyone else at risk. I got lucky. Sometimes you don't." He watched the last of Lopez's yacht sink. "What about our two guests?"

"They're still in the shed."

"Load them up and take them in to Nassau and say we'll file charges for trespassing," Micah told Rodrigo.

"I'm on my way."

"We'll have federal agents combing the island by dawn, I guess," one of the other mercenaries groaned.

Micah shook his head. "I was sanctioned. And that's all I intend to say about this, ever," he added when the man seemed set to protest. "Let's see if we can get a little more sleep before dawn."

Mumbled agreement met the suggestion. He walked back into the house and down the hall to his bedroom. Callie's door was still closed. He felt a horrible pang of guilt when he remembered what had happened before he went after Lopez. He was never going to get over what he'd done.

He took a shower and changed into a pair of white striped shorts and a white-and-red patterned silk shirt. He padded down the hall to the kitchen and started to get a beer out of the refrigerator. But it hadn't been a beer sort of night. He turned on his heel and went to the liquor cabinet in his study. He poured himself two fingers of Kentucky bourbon with a little ice and took it back down the hall with him.

At the door of Callie's room, he paused. He opened the door gently and moved in to stand by the bed and look down at her. She was sound asleep, her cheek pillowed on a pretty hand devoid of jewelry. She'd kicked off the sheet and bedspread and her long legs were visible where the gown had fallen away from them. She looked innocent, untouched. He remembered the feel of that soft mouth under his lips, the exquisite loving that had driven every sane thought out of his mind. His body went rigid just from the memory.

She stirred, as if she sensed his presence, but she didn't wake up. The sedative had really kicked in now. She wouldn't wake until dawn, if then.

He reached down a gentle hand and brushed the hair away from the corner of her mouth and her cheek. She wasn't conventionally pretty, but she had an inner beauty that made him feel as if he'd just found spring after a hard winter. He liked to hear her laugh. He liked the way she dressed, so casually and indifferently. She didn't take hours to put on makeup, hours to dress. She didn't complain about the heat or the cold or the food. She was as honest as any woman he'd ever known. She had wonderful qualities. But he was afraid of her.

He'd been a loner most of his life. His mother's death when he was ten had hit him hard. He'd adored his mother. After that, it had been Jack and himself, and they'd grown very close. But when Callie and her mother moved in, everything had changed. Suddenly he was an outsider in his own family. He despised Callie's mother and made no secret of his resentment for both women. That had caused a huge rift between his father and himself, one that had inevitably grown wide enough to divide them altogether.

He'd blamed Callie for the final blow, because he'd convinced himself that she'd found Jack and sent him to the hall to find Micah and Anna kissing. Callie had always denied it, and finally he believed her. It hadn't been pique because he'd rejected her.

He took a sip of the whiskey and stared down at her broodingly. She was part of his life, part of him. He hated knowing that. He hated the memory of her body moving sensuously under his while he seduced her.

And she thought she was dreaming. What if she woke up still believing that? They'd not only had sex, but thanks to him they'd had unprotected sex. His dark eyes slid down her body to her flat belly. Life might already be growing in her womb.

His breath caught. Callie might have his baby. His lips parted as he thought about a baby. He'd never wanted one before. He could see Callie with an infant in her arms, in her heart, in her life. Callie would want his baby.

He felt an alien passion gripping him for the first time. And just as quickly, he considered the difficulty it would engender. Callie might be pregnant. She wouldn't remember how she got that way, either.

He pursed his lips, feeling oddly whimsical for a man who was facing the loss of freedom and perhaps even the loss of his lifestyle and his job. Wouldn't it be something if Callie was pregnant and he was the only one who knew?

## Chapter Eleven

Callie felt the sun on her face. She'd been dreaming. She'd been in Micah's warm, powerful arms, held tight against every inch of him, and he'd been making ardent love to her. He'd looked down into her wide eyes at the very instant he'd possessed her. He'd watched her become a woman. It seemed so real…

Her eyes opened. Sure it was real. And any minute now, the tooth fairy was going to fly in through the open patio windows and leave her a shiny quarter!

She sat up. Odd, that uncomfortable feeling low in her belly. She shifted and she felt sore. Talk about dreams that seemed real!

She swung her legs off the bed and stood up, stilling for a moment so that the sudden dizziness passed. She turned to make up the bed and frowned. There was a stain on the bottom sheet. It looked like dried blood. Well, so much for the certainty that her period wasn't due for another two weeks, she thought. Probably all the excitement had brought it on sooner. She went into the bathroom, wondering what she was going to do for the necessary equipment in a house full of men.

But she wasn't having her period. That would mean some spotting had occurred and that frightened her because it wasn't natural. She'd always been regular. She'd have to see a doctor when she got home, she supposed.

She bathed and frowned when she was standing in front of the mirror. There were some very bad bruises on her hip and thigh, and that was when she remembered the terror of the night before. Half asleep, she hadn't really been thinking until she saw the bruises and it began to come back. A man, Lopez's man, had tried to kidnap her. She'd actually knocked him out with a shovel. She smiled as she remembered it. Sadly she'd been less brave when Micah came running out to see about her. He'd carried her in here and given her a sedative. She hoped she hadn't said anything revealing to him. Sedatives made her very uninhibited. But she had no memory past the shot. That might, she concluded, be a good thing.

Dressed in a pink Bermuda shorts set that she'd bought on her shopping trip in Nassau, she put her feet into a new pair of sneakers. Unlike the sandals she couldn't wear, the sneakers were a perfect fit.

She walked back into the bedroom worriedly, wondering what Micah had done with Lopez's men. It seemed very quiet this morning. She was certain Micah had all sorts of surveillance systems set up to make sure Lopez couldn't sneak anybody else in here to make another attempt at kidnapping her. But she felt uneasy, just the same. Lopez would never stop. She knew that she was still in the same danger she'd been in when she first arrived here with Micah.

She felt as if she had a hangover, probably because of that sedative Micah gave her. That explained the erotic dream as well. She blushed, remembering what an erotic dream it was, too. She brushed her hair, not bothering with makeup, and went down the hall to the kitchen to see if coffee was available.

Bojo was helping himself to a cup. He grinned as she came into the room. "You slept very late."

"I was very tired. Besides, Micah drugged me. That's the second time he's given me a sedative since I've been here. I'm not used to them." She laughed as she took the fresh cup of coffee Bojo handed her. "It's a good thing I fell asleep right away, too, because sedatives generally have a very odd effect on me. I get totally swept away. Where is everybody?" she added, noting that Bojo was the only person in the house.

"Micah has gone to Nassau on business," he told her with a grin. "Lopez seems to have vanished in the night. Not only Lopez, but his very expensive yacht and several of his men. The authorities are justifiably curious."

"Lopez has gone?" she asked, excited. "You mean, he's gone away?"

"Very far away," he said with a grin.

"But he'll just come back." He gave her a wry look and she frowned. "Don't you still have his two henchmen? Micah was going to give those two men to the police," she reminded him. "Maybe they know where he is."

"They were handed over to the police," he agreed. "But they don't know where Lopez is, either."

"You look smug," she accused.

He smiled. "I am. I do know where Lopez is. And I can promise you that he won't be making any more raids on this island."

"Great!" she exclaimed, relieved. "Can you hand him over to the police, too?"

"Lopez can't be handed over." He paused to think. "Well, not in one piece, at least," he added.

"You're sounding very strange," she pointed out.

He poured his own cup of coffee and sat back down at the table. "Lopez's yacht went up in flames last night," he said matter-of-factly. "I am amazed that you didn't hear the explosion. It must have been a fault in the engine, or a gas leak," he added, without meeting her eyes. He shook his head. "A very nasty explosion. What was left of the yacht sank within sight of here."

"His boat sank? He was on it? You're sure? Did you see it go down?" she asked, relieved and horrified at the same time.

"Yes, yes, and yes." He studied her. "Lopez will never threaten you or Micah's father again. You will be able to return home now, to your job and your stepfather. I shall miss you."

"I'll miss you, too, Bojo," she said, but her mind was racing ahead. Lopez was dead. She was out of danger. She could go home. She had to go home, she amended. She would never see Micah again…

Bojo was watching the expressions chase themselves across her face. She was vulnerable, and besides that, she was in love with Micah. It didn't take much guesswork to figure that out, or to make sense of Micah's strange attitude about her. Obviously the boss knew she was in love with him, and he was trying to be kind while making his position to her clear.

He grimaced. The musical tones of his cell phone interrupted his gloomy thoughts. He answered it quickly.

"Yes," he said, glancing warily at Callie. "She's here, having coffee. I'll ask her." He lifted both eyebrows. "Micah is having lunch with Lisse on the bay in Nassau. If you want to join them, I can take you over in the small boat."

Lisse. Why should she think anything had changed? she wondered. Lisse was beautiful and Micah had told her at the beginning that he and Lisse were lovers. They'd been together for a long time, and she was important in the Bahamas as well as being beautiful. A few teasing kisses for Callie meant nothing to him. She'd been a complete fool. Micah had been kind to her to get her to stay and bait Lopez. That was all it had been. It was an effort to smile, but she did.

"Tell him thanks, but I've got to start packing. If Lopez is really out of the way, I have to go home. Mr. Kemp won't keep my job open forever."

Bojo looked really worried. "Boss, she says she'd rather not." He hesitated, nodded, glanced again at Callie. "Okay. I'll make sure he knows. We'll expect you soon. Yes. Goodbye."

"You look like a bad party," she commented.

"He's bringing Lisse here for lunch," he said reluctantly.

Her heart jumped but she only smiled. "Why not?

It's obvious to anybody that he's crazy about her. She's a dish," she added, and then wondered why she should suddenly think about Lisse's bust size when compared to her own.

"She's a cat," Bojo replied tersely. "Don't let her walk on you."

"I never have," she commented. "If we're having lunch, I guess I need to get started fixing it, huh?"

"We have a cook..."

"I'm good," she told him without conceit. "I cook for Dad and me every night. I'm not *cordon-bleu,* but I get compliments."

"Very well." Bojo gave in, hoping the boss wasn't going to fire him for letting her into the kitchen. "Mac went to Nassau with the boss and the other guys, so it would have been cold cuts anyway."

"I make homemade rolls," she told him with a grin. "And I can bake a pound cake."

She got up, looked through the cupboards and refrigerator, found an apron and got busy. It would give her something to do while her heart was breaking.

Two hours later, Micah and Lisse came into the living room together, laughing. Callie peered out from the kitchen. "Food's on the table if you want to sit down," she called gaily.

Micah gaped at her. He'd told Bojo to get Mac to fix lunch. What was Callie doing in the kitchen?

Bojo came out of it, and Micah's face hardened. "I thought I told you to monitor communications for traffic about Lopez," he said coldly.

Bojo knew what was eating him, so he only

smiled. "I am. I was just asking Callie for another pot of coffee. We drank the other, between us," he added deliberately.

Micah's eyes flashed like black lightning, but he didn't say another word as Bojo nodded politely at Lisse and walked back toward the communications room.

"Sit down, Lisse," Micah said quietly, pulling out a chair for her at the dining-room table, already laid with silverware and plates and fresh flowers. "I'll be back in a minute."

"I do hope it's going to be something light," Lisse said airily. "I can't bear a heavy meal in the middle of the day."

Micah didn't answer her. He'd run into Lisse in town and she'd finagled him into lunch. He'd compromised by bringing her here, so that he could see how Callie was feeling after the night before. He was hoping against hope that she remembered what had happened. But the instant she looked at him, he knew she hadn't.

"Hi," she said brightly and with a forced smile. "I slept like two logs. I hope you've got an appetite. I made homemade bread and cake, and steak and salad."

"Lisse will probably only want the salad," he murmured. "But I love cake."

"I remember. Go sit down. I'll bring it."

"You only set two places," he said quietly.

She shrugged. "I'm just cooking it. I wouldn't want to get in the way...Micah!"

While she was talking, he picked her up and carried her out of the kitchen the back way and into the first sprawling bathroom he came to, closing the door behind them.

"You're not the hired help here," he said flatly, staring into her eyes without putting her down. "You don't wait at table. You don't cook. I have a man for that."

"I'm a good cook," she pointed out. "And it's going to get cold if you don't put me down and let me finish."

His eyes dropped to her mouth and lingered there hungrily. "I don't want food." He brought her close and his mouth suddenly went down against hers and twisted ardently, until he forced her lips apart and made her respond to him. He groaned under his breath as her arms reached up to hold him. She made a husky little sound and gave in all at once. It felt so familiar to be held like this, kissed like this. She opened her mouth and felt his tongue go into it. Her body was on fire. She'd never felt such desire. Odd, that her body seemed to have a whole different knowledge of him than her mind did.

He couldn't get enough of her mouth. He devoured it. His powerful arms had a faint tremor when he was finally able to draw back. He looked straight into her eyes, remembering her headlong response the night before, feeling her body yield to him on crisp, white sheets in the darkness. He'd thought of nothing else all day. It was anguish to know that she was totally oblivious to what they'd done together, when the memories were torturing him.

"How long have you been talking to Bojo?" he demanded gruffly.

"Just…just a little while." Her mouth was swollen, but her body was shivering with secret needs.

She looked at the tight line of his lips and impulsively reached up to kiss him. Amazingly he kissed her back with ardent insistence.

"Micah!" Lisse's strident voice came floating down the hall, followed by the staccato sound of high heels on wood.

Micah heard her and lifted his head. His mouth, like Callie's, was swollen. He searched her misty eyes intently.

"It's Lisse," she whispered dazedly.

"Yes." He bent and brushed his lips lazily over her own, smiling as she followed them involuntarily.

"She wants her lunch," she persisted.

"I want you," he murmured against her mouth.

The words shocked. Her fingers, linked behind his nape, loosened and she looked worried. "I can't!" she whispered huskily.

"Why can't you?"

"Because I've never..." she began.

*Until last night.* He almost said it. He thought it. His face hardened as he forced his tongue to be silent. He couldn't tell her. He wanted to. But it was too soon. He had to show her that it wasn't a one-night thing with him. Even more important, he had to convince himself that he could change enough, settle down enough, to give her some security and stability. He knew that he could have made her pregnant. Oddly it didn't worry him. The thought of a child was magical, somehow. He didn't know much about children, except that he was certain he'd love his own. Callie would make a wonderful mother.

He smiled as he bent and kissed her eyelids shut. "Wouldn't you?" he whispered. "If I insisted?"

"I'd hate you," she bit off, knowing that she wouldn't. She loved him endlessly.

"Yes, you might," he said after a minute. "And that's the last thing I want."

"Micah!" Lisse's voice came again, from even farther down the hall.

"Sit. Stay," Callie whispered impishly.

He bit her lower lip and growled deep in his throat. "She insisted on lunch. I compromised. Kiss me again." His mouth drifted lazily over hers.

She did kiss him, because she had no willpower when it came to this. She loved being in his arms, being held by him. She loved him!

After a minute he lifted his head and put her down, with obvious reluctance. "We'd better go before she starts opening doors," he said in a husky tone.

"Would she?" she asked, curious.

"She has before," he confessed with a wry grin. He brushed back her hair with exquisite tenderness. His eyes held an expression she'd never seen in them. "You look like I've been making love to you," he whispered with a faint smile. "Better fix your face before you come out."

She reached up and touched his swollen mouth with wonder. She was still trying to make herself believe that he'd dragged her in here and kissed her so hungrily. There was something in the back of her mind, something disturbing. She couldn't grasp it. But the most amazing thing was the tenderness he was showing her. It made her breathless.

His lean hand spread against her cheek. His thumb parted her lips as he bent again, as if he couldn't help himself. He kissed her softly, savoring the trembling response of her lips.

*"Micah!"* Lisse was outside, almost screeching now.

He lifted his head again with a long sigh. "I need to take you out in the boat and drop anchor five miles out," he said heavily. He tapped her nose. "Okay, let's go see if everything's cold before Lisse loses her voice."

He opened the door, checking to see if the coast was clear. "Fix your face," he whispered with a wicked grin and closed the door behind him.

She heard his footsteps moving toward the dining room. Two minutes later, staccato heels made an angry sound passing the bathroom door.

"Micah…!"

"I'm in the dining room, Lisse! Where were you? I've been looking everywhere!"

He was good at improvising, Callie thought as she repaired the damage to her face. She combed her hair with a comb from a tray on the vanity table and wondered at the change in her relationship with Micah. He was very different. He acted as if she'd become suddenly important to him, and not in a conventional way. She couldn't help smiling. It was as if her whole life had changed.

She went back into the kitchen and put everything on the table, after checking that the steak had kept warm on the back of the stove. It had.

Micah got up and set a third place at the table, giving Callie a deliberate look. "You eat in here with us," he said firmly, ignoring Lisse's glare.

"Okay." She put out the last of the food, and butter for the rolls, and sat down. "Micah, will you say grace?" she added.

*"Grace?"* Lisse's beautiful face widened into shock.

Micah flashed her a disapproving glance and said a brief prayer. He was digging into the food while Lisse, in her gold-trimmed white pantsuit, was still gaping.

"We're very conventional at home," Callie pointed out.

"And traditional," Micah added. "Tradition is important for families."

"But you don't have a family, really, darling," Lisse protested. She helped herself to a couple of forkfuls of salad and a hint of dressing. "Rolls? Thousands of calories, darling, especially with butter!" she told Micah.

"Callie made them for me, from scratch," he said imperturbably. He bit into one and smiled. "These are good," he said.

Callie shrugged. "It's the only thing I do really well. My mother couldn't boil water." That had slipped out and she looked horrified as she met Micah's eyes.

"I think Micah could do very well without hearing about your tramp of a mother, dear," Lisse said haughtily. "He's suffered enough at her hands already. Who was it she threw you over for, darling, that British earl?"

"She didn't throw me over," Micah said through his teeth.

"But she was staying here with you last year…?"

Callie's eyes exploded. She got up, throwing down her napkin. "Is that true?" she demanded.

"It is, but not the way you're assuming it is," he

said flatly. "Callie, there's something you need to know."

She turned and walked out of the room.

"What the hell was that in aid of?" Micah demanded of Lisse, with real anger.

"You keep secrets, don't you?" she asked with cold delight. "It's dangerous. And she isn't really your sister, either. I got that out of Bojo. You've even slept with her, haven't you, darling?" she added venomously.

Micah threw down his own napkin and got to his feet. *"Bojo!"* he yelled.

The tall Berber came rushing into the room. His boss never raised his voice!

Micah was almost vibrating with rage. "See Lisse back to Nassau. She won't be coming here again," he added with ice dropping from every syllable.

Lisse put down her fork and wiped her mouth before she got leisurely to her feet. She gave him a cool look. "You use people," she accused quietly. "It's always what *you* want, what *you* need. You manipulate, you control, you…use. I loved you," she added in a husky undertone. "But you didn't care. I was handy and good in bed, and that was what mattered to you. When you didn't want me so much anymore, you threw me out. I was only invited over here this time so that you could show your houseguest that she wasn't the only egg in your basket." She gave him a cold smile. "So how does it feel to be on the receiving end for once, Micah? It's your turn. I wish, I really wish, I could stick around to see the result. She doesn't look like the forgiving sort to me. And I'd know, wouldn't I?"

She turned, leaving Bojo to follow her after a complicated glance in Micah's direction. The boss didn't say a word. Not a single word.

Callie was packing with shaking hands. Micah came to the doorway and leaned against it with his hands in his pockets, watching her glumly.

"Nothing to say?" she asked curtly.

"Nothing you'd listen to," he replied. He shrugged. "Lisse just put me in my place. I didn't realize it, but she's right. I do use people. Only I never meant to use you, in any way."

"You said you weren't having an affair with my mother," she accused as she folded a pair of slacks and put them in her case.

"I'm not. I never have." His chest rose and fell heavily. "But you're not in any mood to listen, are you, baby?"

Baby. She frowned. Baby. Why did that word make her uneasy? She looked at him with honest curiosity.

"I called you that," he said quietly. "You don't remember when, do you?"

She sighed, shaking her head.

"It may be just as well," he said, almost to himself. "For now, it's safe for you to go home. Lopez is dead. His top lieutenants died with him. There's no longer any threat to you or to Dad."

"Yes. What a lucky explosion it was," she added, busy with her case.

"It wasn't luck, Callie," he said shortly. "I swam out to the yacht and planted a block of C-4 next to his propeller shaft."

She turned, gasping. Her hands shook as she fumbled the case closed and sat down heavily on the bed.

So that was what they'd been talking about the night before, when Micah had said that "it might work." He could have been killed!

"It was a close call," he added, watching her. "I let myself get caught like a rank beginner. I was too tired to make it back in a loop, so I stopped to rest. One of Lopez's men caught me. Lopez made a lot of threats about what he planned to do to you and Dad, and then he got stupid and had me tied up down below." He extended his arm, showed her his watch, pressed a button, and watched her expression as a knife blade popped out. "Pity his men weren't astute enough to check the watch. They knew what I do for a living, too."

Her eyes were full of horror. Micah had gone after Lopez alone. He'd been captured. If it hadn't been for that watch, he'd be dead. She stared at him as if she couldn't get enough of just looking at him. What difference did it make if he'd had a full-blown affair with her mother? He could be out there with Lopez, in pieces...

She put her face in her hands to hide the tears that overflowed.

He went to the bed and knelt beside her, pulling her wet face into his throat. He smoothed her hair while she clung to him and let the tears fall. It had been such a traumatic week for her. It seemed that her whole life had been uprooted and stranded. Micah could have been dead. Or, last night, she could have been dead. Pride seemed such a petty thing all of a sudden.

"You could have died," she whispered brokenly.

"So could you." He moved, lifting her into his arms. He dropped into a wide cushioned rattan chair and held her close while the anguish of the night before lanced through her slender body like a tangible thing. She clung to him, shivering.

"I wish I'd known what you were planning," she said. "I'd have stopped you, somehow! Even if it was only to save you so you could go to my...my mother."

He wrapped her up even closer and laid his cheek against her hair with a long sigh. "You still don't trust me, do you, honey?" he murmured absently. "I suppose it was asking too much, considering the way I've treated you over the years." He kissed her dark hair. "You go back home and settle into your old routine. Soon enough, this will all seem like just a bad dream."

She rubbed her eyes with her fists, like a small child. Curled against him, she felt safe, cherished, treasured. Odd, to feel like that with a man who was a known playboy, a man who'd already told her that freedom was like a religion to him.

"You'll be glad to have your house to yourself again," she said huskily. "I guess it really cramped your style having me here. With Lisse, I mean."

He chuckled. "I lied."

"Wh...what?"

"I lied about Lisse being my lover now. What was between us was over years ago." He shrugged. "I brought her over here when you arrived as a buffer."

She sat up, staring at him like a curious cat. "A buffer?"

He smiled lazily. His fingers brushed away the tears that were wetting her cheeks. "Bachelors are terrified of virgins," he commented.

"You don't even like me," she protested.

His dark eyes slid down to her mouth, and even farther, over her breasts, down to her long legs. "You have a heart like marshmallow," he said quietly. "You never avoid trouble or turn down people in need. You take in all sorts of strays. Children love you." He smiled. "You scared me to death."

"Past tense?" she asked softly.

"I'm getting used to you." He didn't smile. His dark eyes narrowed. "It hurt me that Lopez got two men onto my property while I was lying in bed asleep. You could have been kidnapped or killed, no thanks to me."

"You were tired," she replied. "You aren't superhuman, Micah."

He drew in a slow breath and toyed with the armhole of her tank top. His fingers brushed against soft, warm flesh and she had to fight not to lean toward them. "I didn't feel comfortable resting while we were in so much danger. It all caught up with me last night."

She was remembering something he'd said. "You were almost too tired to swim back from Lopez's yacht, you said," she recalled slowly. She frowned. "But you'd just been asleep," she added. "How could you have been tired?"

"Oh, that's not a question you should ask yet," he said heavily. "You're not going to like the answer."

"I'm not?"

He searched her eyes for a long moment. All at once, he stood up, taking her with him. "You'd better finish getting your stuff together. I'll put you on a commercial flight home."

She didn't want to go, but she didn't have an excuse to stay. She looked at him as if she were lost and alone, and his face clenched.

"Don't do that," he said huskily. "The idea is to get you out of here as smoothly as possible. Don't invite trouble."

She didn't understand that taut command. But then, she didn't understand him, either. She was avoiding the one question she should be asking. She gave in and asked it. "Why was my mother here?"

"Her husband has cancer," he said simply. "She phoned here and begged for help. It seems the earl is penniless and she does actually seem to love him. I arranged for him to have an unorthodox course of treatment from a native doctor here. They both stayed with me until he got through it." He put his hands in his slacks pockets. "As much as I hate to admit it, she's not the woman she was, Callie," he added. "And she did one other thing that I admired. She phoned your father and told him the truth about you."

Her heart skipped. "What father? What truth?" she asked huskily.

"Your father was going to phone you and ask you to meet him. Did he?"

She moved restlessly back to her packing. "He phoned and left a message. I didn't have anything to say to him, so I didn't call him back."

"He knows that you're his child," he told her. "Your mother sent him your birth certificate. That's why he's trying to contact you. I imagine he wants to apologize. Your mother does, too, to you and Dad, but she told me she wasn't that brave."

Her eyes met his, haunted. "I went through hell because of her and my father," she said in a tight tone. "You don't know...you can't imagine...what it was like!"

"Yes, I can," he said, and he sounded angry. "He's apparently counting his regrets. He never re-married. He doesn't have any children, except you."

"Then he still doesn't have a child," she said through her teeth.

He didn't reply for several long seconds. "I can understand why you feel that way, about him and your mother. I don't blame you. I just thought I'd tell you what I know. It's up to you, what you do or don't do about it."

She folded one last shirt and put it into the case. "Thanks for telling me." She glanced at him. "Lisse wanted to make trouble."

"Yes, she did, and she was entitled. She's right. I did use her, in a way. Your mother left me very embittered about women," he confessed. "I loved my own mother, but I lost her when I was still in grammar school. In later years, your mother was the very worst example of what a wife should be. She made a very bad impression on me."

"On me, too." She closed the case and turned back to him, her eyes trying to memorize his lean face. "I wish you'd liked me, when I lived in your house," she said abruptly. "It would have meant more than you know."

His eyes narrowed. "I couldn't afford to like you, Callie," he said quietly. "Every time I looked at you, I burned like fire inside. You were just a teenager, a virgin. I couldn't take advantage of you that way."

"We could have been friends," she persisted.

He shook his head. "You know we couldn't. You know why."

She grimaced, averting her face. "It's always sex with you, isn't it?"

"Not anymore." His voice was quiet, solemn. "Those days are past. I'm looking ahead now. I have a future to build."

A bigger army of mercenaries, she decided, and more money. She smiled to herself. Once a mercenary, always a mercenary. He'd be the last mercenary who would ever be able to give up the lifestyle.

"I wish you well," she said. She picked up her case and looked around to make sure she hadn't left anything. "Thanks for saving my life. Twice," she added with a forced grin.

"You're welcome." He moved forward to take the case from her. He studied her face for a long time with narrowed eyes. It was as if he was seeing her for the first time. "It's amazing," he murmured involuntarily, "that it took me so long."

"What took you so long?"

"Never mind," he murmured, and he smiled. "You'll find out soon enough. Come on. I'll drive you into Nassau to the airport."

"Bojo could..."

He put his fingers against her soft mouth, and he didn't smile. "I'll drive you."

She swallowed. The tip of his finger was tracing her upper lip, and it was making her knees weak. "Okay," she said.

He took her hand and led her out to the car.

## Chapter Twelve

Two weeks later, Callie was back at work and it was as if she'd never been kidnapped by Lopez's men or gone to Nassau with Micah. Despite the excitement and adventure, she hadn't told anyone except Mr. Kemp the truth about what had happened. And she let him think that Lopez had died in a freak accident, to protect Micah.

Micah had walked her to the concourse and kissed her goodbye in such a strange, breathlessly tender way that it had kept her from sleeping much since she'd been back. The look in his eyes had been fascinating, but she was still trying to decide what she'd seen there. He'd said he'd see her soon. She had no idea what he meant. It was like leaving part of herself behind when she got on the plane. She cried all the way to Miami, where she got on a plane to San Antonio and then a charter flight to Jacobsville from there.

Micah's father was much better, and so glad to see her that he cried, too. She dismissed the nurse who'd been staying with him with gratitude and a check, but the nurse refused the check. She'd already been paid her fee, in advance, she told a mystified Callie. She left, and Callie and Jack Steele settled back into their comfortable routine.

"I feel better than I have in years," Jack Steele told her with a grin at supper one evening. "It makes me proud that my son wanted to protect me as well as you."

"Micah loves you terribly," she assured him. "He just has a hard time showing it, that's all."

"You really think so?"

"I do. I'm sure he'll come and see you, if you'll let him."

He gave her a peculiar look and pursed his lips. "I'll let Micah come here if you'll do something for me."

"What?"

He leaned back in his chair, and his features reminded her of Micah in a stubborn mood. "If you'll make peace with your father," he said.

She let out a surprised gasp.

"I knew you'd take it like that," he said. "But he's phoned here every single day since you left. He told me some cock-and-bull story about a drug dealer named Lopez. He said he'd heard from a friend in law enforcement that Lopez had kidnapped you and taken you to Mexico. I thought he was full of bull and I told him so. But he kept phoning. I guess it was a good excuse to mend fences. A man that persistent should at least have a hearing.''

She gaped at him. ''You...didn't believe him, about Lopez?''

Her tone surprised him. ''No, of course not.'' Her expression was very disturbing. He scowled. ''Callie...it wasn't true? You really did go to take care of that aunt Micah told me about?''

''Jack, I don't have a aunt,'' she said heavily. ''Lopez did kidnap me. Micah came and got me out himself. He went right into Lopez's house and rescued me.''

''My son, storming drug dealers' lairs?'' he exclaimed. ''Are you kidding?''

''Oh, I didn't want you to have to find out like this,'' she groaned. ''I should have bitten my tongue through!''

He was shocked. ''Micah got you out,'' he repeated.

She leaned across the table and took his arthritic hands in hers and held them tight. ''There's no easy way to say this, but you'll have to know. I'm not sure Micah wants you to know, but I don't have a choice anymore. Dad, Micah is a professional mercenary,'' she told him evenly. ''And he's very good at it. He rappelled from Lopez's roof right into a bedroom and rescued me from a man who was going to kill me. We're both fine. He got me away and out of the country, and took me home with him to Nassau. He lured Lopez in, and...Lopez's boat was blown up in a freak accident.''

Jack let out the breath he'd been holding. ''The things you learn about people you thought you knew. My own son, and he never told me.''

She grimaced. "I'm not sure he ever would. He's very brave, Jack. He isn't really money-hungry, although it sounds as if he is. I'd never have survived without him. His men are just the same, dedicated professionals who really care about what they do. They're not a gang of thugs."

Jack sat back in his chair again, scowling. "You know, it does make some sort of sense. He came home bandaged, you remember that time? And he said he'd had a bad fall. But I saw him accidentally without the bandage and it looked like a bullet wound to me."

"It probably was," she said. "He has scars on his back, too."

She frowned, trying to understand how she knew that. She'd seen Micah with his shirt unbuttoned in Nassau, but never with it off completely. How would she know he had scars down his back?

She put that thought out of her mind. "There's something else I found out," she added. "My mother was there last year, staying with him."

Jack's face hardened at once.

"No, it's not what you're thinking," she said quickly. "That was my thought, too, but she asked Micah for help. She's married to a British earl who has cancer. There was a clinic near Micah and he let them stay with him while the earl was treated. He's impoverished, and I suspect that Micah paid for the treatments, too, although he didn't admit it." She smiled. "He says Mother is really in love this time. She wanted to make peace with both of us as well, but she didn't think it would be possible."

"Not for me," Jack said quietly. "She cost me a lot."

"She cost me more," she agreed. "But you can't hate people forever. It only hurts you in the end. You have to forgive unless you want to live in torment forever."

"How did you get so wise, at your age?" he asked, smiling as he tried to lighten the mood.

"I had a lot of hard knocks. I learned early how terrible a thing hatred is." She touched his hand gently. "Micah loves you so much. You can't imagine how it hurt him when we thought he'd betrayed you with Mother. He's been bitter, too."

"I wouldn't let him talk about it," he said. "I should have listened. He's never lied to me, except maybe by omission." He sighed with a wry smile. "I never would have guessed he'd have been in such a profession."

She laughed. "Neither would I." She sighed. "He can't give it up, of course. He told me he had no ambition whatsoever to settle down and have a family. I never really saw him as a family man."

He studied her curiously. "But you wish he was," he said perceptibly.

Her gaze fell to the table. "I love him," she said heavily. "I always have. But he's got all the women in his life that he needs already. Beautiful women. One of them took me shopping when we first got to Nassau."

"You have ties with him that no other woman will ever have. If he didn't care about you, he certainly wouldn't have risked his own life to rescue you," he remarked.

"He did it for you, because he knows you love me," she said. "That's why."

He pursed his lips and his eyes narrowed as he studied her. "Think so? I wonder."

She got up. "I'll fix dinner. Then I guess I'll try to phone my father."

"Remember what you said, about forgiving people, Callie," he reminded her. "Your mother told him a lot of lies. He believed her, but maybe it was easier to believe her, when he knew she was taking you away. He was going to lose you anyway."

"She didn't take me away," she said coldly. "He threw me out, and she put me in foster care immediately."

He grimaced. "Yes, I know. Your father told me. He'd only just found out."

"Found out, how?" she exclaimed.

"Apparently he hired a private detective," he said gently. "He was appalled at how you'd been treated, Callie. He blames himself."

She moved restlessly, her eyes glancing at him. "You're the only father I've ever known."

He grinned. "You'll always have me. But give the man a chance. He's not as bad as you remember him being." The smile faded. "Maybe, like your mother, he's found time to face himself and his mistakes."

She turned away. "Okay. I guess it wouldn't hurt to talk to him."

She phoned, but her father was out of the country. She left a message for him on his answering machine, a stumbling sort of greeting and her phone number. If he hadn't given up on her, he might try again.

The next week dragged. She missed Micah. She felt tired. She wondered if all the excitement of the past few weeks wasn't catching up with her. She also seemed to have stopped having a period. She'd always been regular and never skipped, and then she remembered that odd spotting in Nassau. She grimaced. It must be some sort of female problem. She'd have to make an appointment to see Dr. Lou Coltrain.

She made the appointment from work, just after she got back from lunch. When she hung up, her boss, Blake Kemp, was speaking to someone in his office, the door just having opened so that he could show his client out.

"...yes, he phoned me a couple of days ago," the client was saying. "He used to hate Jacobsville, which makes it even stranger. We were all shocked."

"Yes," Kemp replied. "He had a whole island, didn't he? He's already sold up there, and he's got big plans for the Colbert Ranch property. He owns several thoroughbreds, which he's having shipped here from New Providence. He plans to have one of the best racing stables in Texas, from what he says."

"He says he's giving up the business as well and coming back here to live."

"That's another odd thing, he mentioned going back to medical school and finishing his residency," Kemp chuckled.

"He's good at what he used to do. He's patched me up enough over the years." The tall man with the green eyes, favoring a burned forearm and hand glanced at Callie and noted her shocked face. "Yes, Callie, I'm talking about your stepbrother. I don't guess you and Jack Steele knew a thing about this, did you?"

She shook her head, too stunned to speak.

"That's like Micah." The client chuckled. "He always was secretive. Well, Callie, you look none the worse for wear after your ordeal."

She finally realized who the client was. That was Cy Parks! She knew that he and Micah were friends, but until recently she hadn't known that they shared the same profession.

"Micah's moving here?" she asked involuntarily.

"He is," Cy told her. "But don't tell him you heard me say so," he added with a twinkle in his green eyes. "I don't need to lose any more teeth."

"Sure thing, Mr. Parks," she said with a smile.

"He couldn't stop talking about how brave you were, you know," he added unexpectedly. "He was so proud of you."

She flushed. "He never said so."

"He doesn't, usually." He smiled. "Your father will enjoy having him home, too."

She nodded. "He's proud of Micah. I had to tell him the truth. He'll be over the moon to think that Micah's coming home. He's missed him."

"That cuts both ways. I'm glad to see him making an attempt to settle down," he added with a chuckle. "I can recommend it highly. I never expected so much happiness in my own life. Lisa's pregnant, you know," he added. "It's going to be a boy. We're both over the moon."

"Babies are nice," Callie said wistfully. "Thanks for telling me about Micah, Mr. Parks."

"Make it Cy," he told her. "I expect we'll be seeing each other again. Kemp, walk me out, I want to ask you something."

"Sure thing."

The men walked out onto the sidewalk and Callie

stared at her computer screen with trembling fingers on the keyboard. Micah had sold his island. He was coming to live in Jacobsville. Was Lisse coming with him? Had they made up in spite of what he'd said about her? Was he going to marry the beautiful blonde and set up housekeeping here? If he was, she couldn't bear to stay in Jacobsville!

She felt like bawling. Her emotions had been all over the place lately. Along with the sudden bouts of fatigue and an odd nausea at night, and a missing period, she was likely to cry at the drop of a hat. She remembered a girlfriend having all those same symptoms, but of course, the girlfriend had been pregnant. That wasn't possible in her case. An erotic dream did not produce conception, after all. She was going to see the doctor the next day, anyway. She'd know what was wrong then, if anything was. She hoped it was nothing too terrible.

When she got home that evening, the doctor, the office, everything went right out of her head. There was a black Porsche convertible sitting in the driveway. With her heart pounding like mad, she got out and rushed up the front steps and into the apartment house.

She opened her own door, which was unlocked, and there was Micah, sitting at the dining-room table with Jack Steele while they shared a pot of coffee.

"Micah!" she exclaimed, everything she felt showing helplessly on her face.

He got to his feet, his face somber and oddly watchful. "Hello, Callie," he said quietly.

"I thought...I mean, I didn't think..." The room

was swirling around her. She felt an odd numbness in her face and everything went white.

Micah rushed forward and caught her up in his arms before she hit the floor.

"Her bedroom's through there," Jack told him. "She's been acting very odd, lately. Tired and goes to bed early. I'll make another pot of coffee."

"Thanks, Dad."

Micah carried her to her room and laid her down gently on the white coverlet of her bed. Her fingers were like ice. He brushed back her disheveled hair and his heart clenched at just the sight of her. He'd missed her until it was anguish not to hear her voice, see her face.

She moaned and her eyes opened slowly, looking up into his. She was faintly nauseous and her throat felt tight.

"I feel awful, Micah," she whispered. "But I'm so happy to see you!"

"I'm happy to see you, too," he replied, but he didn't look it. He looked worried. His big hand flattened on her belly, resting there very gently. He leaned close and his lips touched her eyelids, closing them. They moved down her face, over her cheeks, to her soft lips and he kissed her with breathless tenderness. "Callie," he whispered, and his lips became hard and insistent, as if he couldn't help himself.

She opened her mouth to him unconsciously, and her arms went around his neck, pulling him down. She forgot about Lisse, about everything. She kissed him back hungrily. All the weeks apart might never have been. She loved him so!

After a long minute, he forced himself to lift his head. He drew in a long, hard breath. He looked down where his hand was resting on her belly. It wasn't swollen yet, but he was certain, somehow, that she was carrying his child.

"Why...are you doing that?" she asked, watching his hand smooth over her stomach.

"I don't know how to tell you," he replied gently. "Callie...do you remember the night Lopez's men tried to kidnap you again? Do you remember that I gave you a sedative?"

"Yes," she said, smiling nervously.

"And you had an...erotic dream," he continued.

"Yes." She shifted on the cover. "I'd rather not talk about it."

"But we have to. Callie, I..."

"How about some coffee?" Jack Steele asked, poking his head through the doorway. "I just made a fresh pot."

"I'd like some," Callie said with a forced smile. "I'd like something to eat, too. I'm so empty!"

"That's what you think," Micah said under his breath. He stared down at her with twinkling eyes and a smile unlike any smile she'd ever seen on his lips before.

"You look very strange," she commented.

He shrugged. "Don't I always?"

She laughed gently. "Cy Parks was in Mr. Kemp's office today," she said as he helped her to her feet. "He said you were moving here...oops! I promised not to say anything, too. Please don't get mad at him, Micah."

"It's no big secret," he said gently. "In small towns, everybody knows what's going on. It's all right."

"You really are coming back here?"

Her wide eyes and fascinated expression made him tingle all over. "I am. I'm going to breed thoroughbreds. It's something I've always had an interest in. I might finish my residency as well. Jacobsville can always use another doctor."

"I guess so. I have to go see Dr. Lou Coltrain tomorrow. I think I may have a female problem," she said absently as they started out of the bedroom.

"Tomorrow?"

"After lunch," she said. "Don't tell Dad," she said, holding him back by the sleeve before they left the room. "I don't want him to worry. It probably scared him when I fainted. It scared me, too," she confessed.

He touched her hair gently. He wanted to tell her, but he didn't know how. He needed to talk to Lou Coltrain first. This had to be done very carefully, so that Callie didn't feel he was being forced into a decision he didn't want to make.

She searched his eyes. "You look so tired, Micah," she said softly.

"I don't sleep well since you left the island," he replied. "I've worried about you."

"I'm doing okay," she said at once, wanting to reassure him. "I don't even have nightmares." She looked down at her hand on his sleeve. "Micah, is Lisse…I mean, will she come, too?"

"Lisse is history. I told you that when you left. I meant it."

"She's so beautiful," she said huskily.

He frowned, tipping her face up to his with a hand under her chin. "You're beautiful yourself. Didn't you know?" he asked tenderly. "You have this big, open heart that always thinks of other people first.

You have a generosity of spirit that makes me feel selfish by comparison. You glow, Callie.'' He smiled softly. ''That's real beauty, the kind you don't buy in the cosmetic section of the department store. Lisse can't hold a candle to you.'' The smile faded. ''No woman on earth could, right now. You're pure magic to me, Callie. You're the whole world.''

That sounded serious. She just stared at him, transfixed, while she tried to decipher what he was saying.

''Coffee?'' Jack Steele repeated, a little more loudly.

They both jumped when they saw him there. Then they laughed and moved out of the bedroom. Jack poured coffee into mugs and Micah carried Callie hers.

''Feeling better?'' Jack asked.

''Oh, yes,'' she said, the excitement she was feeling so plain on her face that Micah grinned. ''Much better!''

Micah stayed near Callie for the rest of the evening, until he had to go. She'd fixed them a meal and had barely been able to eat a bite of it. She had little appetite, but mostly she was too excited. Micah was watching her as if everything she did fascinated him. All her dreams of love seemed to be coming true. She couldn't believe the way he was looking at her. It made her tingle.

She walked out with him after he'd said his goodnights to his father. ''You could stay,'' she said.

''I can't sleep on that dinky little sofa, and Dad's in a twin bed. So unless you're offering to share your nice big double bed...?'' he teased as they paused by the driver's side of his car.

She flushed. "Stop that."

He touched her cheek with his fingertips. "There's something I wanted to ask you. I can't seem to find a way to do it."

"What? You can ask me anything," she said softly.

He bent and brushed his mouth over hers. "Not yet. Come here and kiss me."

"We have neighbors…" she protested weakly.

But he'd already lifted her clear of the ground and he was kissing her as if there was no tomorrow. She held on and kissed him back with all her might. Two young boys on skateboards went whizzing by with long, insinuating wolf whistles.

Micah lifted his head and gave them a hard glare. "Everyone's a critic," he murmured.

"I'm not complaining," she whispered. "Come back here…"

He kissed her again and then, reluctantly, put her back on her feet. "Unless you want to make love on the hood of the car, we'd better put on the brakes." He looked around. More people had appeared. Incredible that there would be hordes of passersby at this hour in a small Texas town. He glared at two couples sauntering by. They grinned.

"That's Mr. and Mrs. Harris, and behind them is Mr. Harris's son and Jill Williams's daughter. They're going steady," she explained. "They know me, but I'm not in the habit of being kissed by handsome men in Porsches. They're curious."

He nodded over her shoulder. "And her?"

She followed where he was looking. "That's old Mrs. Smith. She grows roses."

"Yes. She seems to be pruning them." He

checked his watch. "Ten o'clock at night is an odd hour to do that, isn't it?"

"Oh, she just doesn't want to look as if she's staring," she explained. "She thinks it would embarrass us." She added in a whisper, "I expect she thinks we're courting."

He twirled a strand of dark hair around his fingers. "Aren't we?" he asked with a gentle smile.

"Courting?" She sounded breathless. She couldn't help it.

He nodded. "You're very old-fashioned, Callie. In some ways, so am I. But you'd better know up-front that I'm not playing."

"You already said you didn't want to settle down," she said, nodding agreement.

"That isn't what I mean."

"Then what do you mean?"

"Hello, Callie!" came an exuberant call from the window upstairs. It was Maria Ruiz, who was visiting her aunt who lived upstairs. She was sixteen and vivacious. "Isn't it a lovely night?"

"Lovely."

"Who's the dish?" the younger woman asked with an outrageous grin. "He's a real hunk. Does he belong to you, or is he up for grabs?"

"Sorry, I'm taken," Micah told her.

"Just my luck," she sighed. "Well, good night!"

She closed the window and the curtain and went back inside.

Callie laughed softly. "She's such a doll. She looks in on Dad when her aunt's working. I told you about her aunt, she doesn't speak any English."

He bent again and kissed her lazily. "You taste like roses," he whispered against her mouth. He enfolded her against him, shivering a little as his body responded instantly to the feel of hers against it and began to swell. He groaned softly as he kissed her again.

"Micah, you're..." She felt the hard crush of his mouth and she moaned, too. It was as if she'd felt him like this before, but in much greater intimacy. It was as if they'd been lovers. She held on tight and kissed him until she was shivering, too.

His mouth slid across her cheek to her ear, and he was breathing as roughly as she was. "I want you," he bit off, holding her bruisingly close. "I want you so much, Callie!"

"I'm sorry," she choked. "I can't...!"

He took deep breaths, trying to keep himself in check. He had to stop this. It was too soon. It was much too soon.

"It may not seem like it, but I'm not asking you to," he said. "It's just that there are things you don't know, Callie, and I don't know how to tell them to you."

"Bad things?"

He let out a slow breath. "Magical things," he whispered, cradling her in his arms as he thought about the baby he was certain she was carrying. His eyes closed as he held her. "The most magical sort of things. I've never felt like this in my life."

She wanted, so much, to ask him what he was feeling. But she was too shy. Perhaps if she didn't push him, he might like her. He sounded as if he did. She smiled, snuggling close to him, completely un-intimidated with the hard desire of his body. She loved making him feel this way.

He smoothed over her hair with a hand that wasn't

quite steady. His body ached, and even that was
sweet. The weeks without her had been pure hell.

"Soon," he said enigmatically. "Very soon."

"What?"

He kissed her hair. "Nothing. I'd better go. Mrs.
Smith is cutting the tops off the roses. Any minute
now, there won't even be a bud left."

She glanced past his shoulder. She giggled helplessly. The romantic old woman was so busy watching them that she was massacring her prize roses!

"She wins ribbons for them, you know," she murmured.

"She won't have any left."

"She's having the time of her life," she whispered. "Her boyfriend married her sister. They
haven't spoken in thirty years and she's never even
looked at another man. She reads romance novels
and watches movies and dreams. This is as close as
she's likely to get to a hot romance. Even if it isn't."

"It certainly is," he whispered wickedly. "And if
I don't get out of here *very* soon, she's going to see
more than she bargained for. And so are you."

"Really?" she teased.

His hand slid to the base of her spine and pushed
her close to him. His eyes held a very worldly
amusement at her gasp. "Really," he whispered. He
bent and kissed her one last time. "Go inside."

She forced herself to step back from him. "What
about Bojo and Peter and Rodrigo and Pogo and
Maddie?" she asked suddenly.

"Bojo was being groomed to take over the group.
He's good at giving orders, and he knows how we
operate. I'll be a consultant."

"But why?" she asked, entranced. "And why come back to Jacobsville to raise horses?"

"When you're ready for those answers I'll give them to you," he said with a gentle smile. "But not tonight. I'll be in touch. Good night."

He was in the car and gone before she could get another word out. Several doors down, Mrs. Smith was muttering as she looked at the rosebuds lying heaped around her feet. The skateboarders went past again with another round of wolf whistles. The couples walking gave her long, wicked grins. Callie went back inside, wondering if she should give them all a bow before she went inside.

## Chapter Thirteen

Micah was ushered back into Dr. Lou Coltrain's office through the back door, before she started seeing her patients. He shook hands with her and took the seat she indicated in her office. She sat down behind her desk, blond and attractive and amused.

"Thanks for taking time to see me this morning," he said. He noted her wry look and chuckled. "Is my head on backward?" he asked.

"You may wish it was," she replied with twinkling dark eyes. "I think I know why you're here. At least two people have hinted to me that Callie Kirby's having what sounds like morning sickness."

He sighed and smiled. "Yes."

"And you're the culprit, unless I miss my guess. Are you here to discuss alternatives?" she asked, suddenly serious.

"I am not!" he said at once. "I want a baby as much as Callie will, when she knows about it."

"When she knows? She doesn't suspect?" she asked, wide-eyed.

He grimaced. "Well, it's like this. Lopez and his thugs—you know about them?" When she nodded, he sighed. "I was careless and they almost got her a second time in Nassau. She knocked her assailant out with a shovel, but she was really shaken up afterward. I gave her a sedative." His high cheekbones colored and he averted his eyes. "She got amorous and I was already upset and on the edge, and I'd abstained for so damned long. And...well..."

"Then what?" she asked, reading between the lines with avid curiosity.

He shifted in the chair, still avoiding eye contact. "She doesn't remember anything. She thinks it was an erotic dream."

Her intake of breath was audible. "In all my years of medicine..." she began.

"I haven't had that many, but it's news to me, too. The thing is, I'm sure she's pregnant, but she'll have a heart attack if you tell her she is. I have to break it to her. But first I have to find a way to convince her to marry me," he added. "So that she won't spend the rest of our lives together believing that the baby forced me into marriage. It's not like that," he said. He rubbed at a spot on his slacks so that he wouldn't have to meet Lou's intent stare. "She's everything. Everything in the world."

Lou smiled. He wasn't saying the words, but she was hearing them. He loved Callie. So it was like that. The mercenary was caught in his own trap. And, amazingly, he didn't want to get out of it. He wanted the baby!

"What do you want me to do?" she asked.

"I want you to do a blood test and see if she really is pregnant. But if she is, I want you to make some excuse about the results being inconclusive, and you can give her a prescription for some vitamins and ask her to come back in two weeks."

"She'll worry that it's something fatal," Lou advised. "People do."

"Tell her you think it's stress, from her recent ordeal," he persisted. "Please," he added, finding the word hard to say even now. "I just need a little time."

"Just call me Dr. Cupid Coltrain," she murmured. "I guess I'll get drummed out of the AMA, but how can I say no?"

"You're in the business of saving lives," he reminded her. "This will save three of them."

"I hear you're moving back here," she said.

"I am. I'm going to raise thoroughbreds," he added, smiling. "And act as a consultant for Eb Scott when he needs some expertise. That way, I'll not only settle down, I'll have enough of a taste of the old life to satisfy me if things get dull. I might even finish my residency and hit you and Coltrain up for a job."

"Anytime," she said, grinning. "I haven't had a day off in two years. I'd like to take my son to the zoo and not have to leave in the middle of the lions on an emergency call."

He chuckled. "Okay. That's a dare."

She stood up when he did and shook hands again. "You're not what I expected, Mr. Steele," she said after a minute. "I had some half-baked idea that you'd never give up your line of work, that you'd want Callie to do something about the baby."

"I do. I want her to have it," he said with a smile. "And a few more besides, if we're lucky. Callie and I were only children. I'd like several, assorted."

"So would we, but one's all we can handle at the moment. Of course, if you finish your residency and stand for your medical license, that could change," she added, tongue-in-cheek.

He grinned. "I guess it's contagious."

She nodded. "Very. Now get out of here. I won't tell Callie I've ever seen you in my life."

"Thanks. I really mean it."

"Anything for a future colleague," she returned with a grin of her own.

Callie worried all morning about the doctor's appointment, but she relaxed when she was in Lou's office and they'd drawn blood and Lou had checked her over.

"It sounds to me like the aftereffects of a very traumatic experience," Lou said with a straight face. "I'm prescribing a multiple vitamin and I want you to come back and see me in two weeks."

"Will the tests take that long?" Callie asked.

"They might." Lou sighed. "You're mostly tired, Callie. You should go to bed early and eat healthy. Get some sun, too. And try not to worry. It's nothing serious, I'm positive of that."

Callie smiled her relief. "Thanks, Dr. Coltrain!" she said. "Thanks, so much!"

"I hear your stepbrother's moving back to town,'

Lou said as she walked Callie to the door of the cubicle. "I guess you'll be seeing a lot of him now."

Callie flushed. "It looks that way." Her eyes lit up. "He's so different. I never could have imagined Micah settling for small-town life."

"Men are surprising people," Lou said. "You never know what they're capable of."

"I suppose so. Well, I'll see you in two weeks."

"Count on it," Lou said, patting her on the shoulder. "Lots of rest. And take those vitamins," she added, handing over the prescription.

Callie felt as if she were walking on air. No health problems, just the aftereffects of the kidnapping. That was good news indeed. And when Micah phoned and asked her to come out to the ranch with him and see the house, she was over the moon.

He picked her up after work at her apartment house. "I took Dad out there this morning," he told her with a grin. "He's going to move in with me at the weekend."

Callie's heart jumped. "This weekend?"

He nodded, glancing at her. "You could move in, too."

Her heart jumped, but she knew he didn't mean that the way it sounded. "I like living in town," she lied.

He smiled to himself. He knew what she was refusing. She wasn't about to live in sin with him in Jacobsville, Texas.

He reached for her hand and linked her fingers with his. "Did you go see the doctor?"

"Yes. She said it was stress. I guess it could be. At least, it's nothing extreme."

"Thank God," he said.

"Yes."

He turned down onto a long winding graveled road. Minutes later, they pulled up in front of a big white Victorian house with a turret room and a new tin roof. "It's really old-fashioned and some of the furniture will have to be replaced," he said, helping her out of the car. "But it's got potential. There's a nice rose garden that only needs a little work, and a great place out to the side for a playground. You know, a swing set and all those nice plastic toys kids love so much."

She stared at him. "You have kids?" she asked with an impish smile.

"Well, not yet," he agreed. "But they're definitely in the picture. Don't you like kids?" he asked with apparent carelessness.

"I love them," she said, watching him warily. "I didn't think you did."

He smiled. "I'll love my own, Callie," he said, his fingers contracting in hers. "Just as you'll love them."

"I'll love your kids?" she blurted out.

He couldn't quite meet her eyes. He stared down toward the big barn a few hundred yards behind the house and he linked his fingers tighter with hers. "Have you ever thought," he said huskily, "about making a baby with me?"

Her heart went right up into her throat. She flushed scarlet. But it wasn't embarrassment. It was pure, wild, joy.

He looked down at her then. Everything she thought, felt, was laid out there for him to see. He caught his breath at the depth of those emotions she didn't know he could see. It was more than he'd ever dared hope for.

"I want a baby, Callie," he whispered huskily. He framed her red face in his hands and bent to kiss her eyelids closed. His fingers were unsteady as he held her where he wanted her, while his mouth pressed tender, breathless little kisses all over her soft skin. "I want one so much. You'd make...the most wonderful little mother," he bit off, choked with emotion. "I could get up with you in the night, when the baby cried, and take turns walking the floor. We could join the PTA later. We could make memories that would last us forever, Callie—you and me and a little boy or a little girl."

She slid her arms tight under his and around him and held on for dear life, shaking with delighted surprise. He wasn't joking. He really meant it. Her eyes closed. She felt tears pouring down her cheeks.

He felt them against his thin silk shirt and he smiled as he reached in his pocket for a handkerchief. He drew her away from him and dabbed at the tears, bending to kiss away the traces. "We can build a big playground here," he continued, as if he hadn't said anything earthshaking. "Both of us were only kids. I think two or three would be nice. And Dad would love being a grandfather. He can stay with us and the kids will make him young again."

"I'd love that. I never dreamed you'd want to have a family or settle down. You said..."

He kissed the words back against her lips. "Freedom is only a word," he told her solemnly. "It stopped meaning anything to me when I knew that Lopez had you." The memory of that horror was suddenly on his face, undisguised. "I couldn't rest until I knew where you were. I planned an assault in a day that should have taken a week of preparation. And then I went in after you myself, because I couldn't trust anyone to do it but me.'' His hands clenched on her shoulders. ''When I saw you like that, saw what that animal had done to you...'' He stopped and swallowed hard. ''My God, if he'd killed you, I'd have cut him to pieces! And then,'' he whispered, folding her close, shivering with the depth of his feelings, ''I'd have picked you up in my arms and I'd have jumped off the balcony into the rocks with you. Because I wouldn't want to live in a world...that didn't hold us both. I couldn't live without you. Not anymore.''

There was a faint mist in his black eyes. She could barely see it for the mist in her own. She choked on a sob as she looked up at him. ''I love you,'' she whispered brokenly. ''You're my whole life. I never dared to hope that you might care for me, too!''

He folded her against him and held her close, rocking her, his cheek on her dark hair as he counted his blessings. They overwhelmed him. She loved him. His eyes closed. It seemed that love could forgive anything, even his years of unkindness. ''I wish I could take back every single hurtful thing I've ever done or said to you.''

She smiled tearfully against his broad chest. ''It's all right, Micah. Honest it is. Do you really want babies?'' she asked dreamily, barely aware of anything he'd said.

''More than anything in the world!''

''I won't sleep with you unless you marry me,'' she said firmly.

He chuckled. ''I'll marry you as soon as we can

get a license. But," he added on a long sigh, drawing back, "I'm afraid it's too late for the sleeping together part."

Her thin eyebrows arched up. "What?"

He traced around her soft lips. "Callie, that erotic dream you had..." He actually flushed. "Well, it wasn't a dream," he added with a sheepish grin.

Her eyes widened endlessly. All those explicit things he'd done and said, that she'd done and said, that had seemed like something out of a fantasy. The fatigue, the spotting, the lack of a period, the...

"Oh my God, I'm pregnant!" she exclaimed in a high-pitched tone.

"Oh my God, yes, you are, you incredible woman!" he said with breathless delight. "I'm sorry, but I went to Lou Coltrain behind your back and begged her not to tell you until we came to an understanding. I was scared to death that you'd be off like a shot if you knew it too soon." He shook his head at her surprise. "I've never wanted anything as much as I want this child—except you," he added huskily. "I can't make it without you, Callie. I don't want to try." He glanced around them at the house and the stable. "This is where we start. You and me, a new business, a new life—in more ways than one," he added with a tender hand on her soft abdomen. "I know I'm something of a risk. But I'd never have made the offer to come here unless I'd been sure, very sure, that I could make it work. I want you more than I want the adventure and the freedom. I love you with all my heart. Is that enough?"

She smiled with her heart in her eyes. "It's enough," she said huskily.

He seemed to relax then, as if he'd been holding

his breath the whole while. His eyes closed and he shivered. "Thank God," he said reverently.

"You didn't think I was going to say no?" she asked, shocked. "Good Lord, the sexiest man in town offers me a wedding ring and you think I'm going to say no?"

He pursed his lips. "Sexy, huh?"

"You seduced me," she pointed out. "Only a very sexy man could have managed that." She frowned. "Of course, you did drug me first," she added gleefully.

"You were hysterical," he began.

"I was in love," she countered, smiling. "And I wasn't all that sedated." She blushed. "But I did think it was a dream. You see, I'd had sort of the same dream since I was...well, since I was about sixteen."

His lips parted on a shocked breath. "That long?"

She nodded. "I couldn't even get interested in anybody else. But you didn't want me..."

"I did want you," he countered. "That's why I was horrible to you. But never again," he promised huskily. "Never again. I'm going to work very hard at being a good husband and father. You won't regret it, Callie. I swear you won't."

"I know that. You won't regret it, either," she promised. She placed her hand over his big one, that still lay gently against her stomach. "And I never guessed," she whispered, smiling secretly. Her eyes brimmed over with excitement. "I'm so happy," she told him brokenly. "And so scared. Babies don't come with instruction manuals."

"We have Lou Coltrain, who's much better than an instruction manual," he pointed out with a grin.

"And speaking of Lou, did you get those vitamins she prescribed?"

"Well, not yet," she began.

"They're prenatal vitamins," he added, chuckling. "You're going to be amazed at how good you feel. Not to mention how lucky you are," he added blithely, "to have a husband who knows exactly what to expect all through your pregnancy." He kissed her softly. "After the baby comes, I might finish my residency and go into practice with the Coltrains," he added.

That meant real commitment, she realized. He was giving up every vestige of the old life for her. Well, almost. She knew he'd keep his hand in with Eb Scott's operation. But the last of Jacobsville's mercenaries was ready to leave the past behind and start again.

So many beautiful memories are about to be created here, she thought as she looked around her from the shelter of Micah's hard arms. She pressed close with a sigh. "After the pain, the pleasure," she whispered.

"What was that?"

"Nothing. Just something I heard when I was younger." She didn't add that it was something her father had said. That was the one bridge she hadn't yet crossed. It would have to be faced. But, she thought, clinging to Micah in the warmth of the sun, not right now...

Micah drove her by the pharmacy on the way back to her apartment. He stood with her while Nancy, the dark-haired, dark-eyed pharmacist filled the prescription, trying not to grin too widely at the picture they made together.

"I suppose you know what these are for?" Nancy asked Callie.

Callie smiled and looked up at Micah, who smiled back with the same tenderness. "Oh, yes," she said softly.

He pulled her close for an instant, before he offered his credit card to pay for them. "We're getting married Sunday at the Methodist church," Micah told her and the others at the counter. "You're all invited…2:00 p.m. sharp."

Nancy's eyes twinkled. "We, uh, heard that from the minister already," she said, clearing her throat as Callie gaped at her.

Micah chuckled at Callie's expression. "You live in a small town, and you didn't think everybody would know already?"

"But you hadn't told me yet!" she accused.

He shrugged. "It didn't seem too smart to announce that I'd arranged a wedding that you hadn't even agreed to yet."

"And they say women keep secrets!" she said on a rough breath.

"Not half as good as men do, sweetheart," Micah told her gently. He glanced around at a sudden commotion behind them. The two remaining bachelor Hart brothers, Rey and Leo, were almost trampling people in their rush to get to the prescription counter.

"Have to have this as soon as possible, sorry!" Rey exclaimed, pressing a prescription into Nancy's hands with what looked like desperation.

"It's an emergency!" Leo seconded.

Nancy's eyes widened. She looked at the brothers with astonishment. "An emergency? This is a prescription for anti-inflammatories…"

''For our cook,'' Leo said. ''Her hands hurt, she said. She can't make biscuits. We rushed her right over to Lou Coltrain and she said it was arthritis.'' He grimaced. ''*Pleaaase* hurry? We didn't get any breakfast at all!''

Callie had her hand over her mouth trying not to have hysterics. Micah just looked puzzled. Apparently he didn't know about the famous biscuit mania.

Leo sounded as if he was starving. Amazing, a big, tall man with a frame like that attempting to look emaciated. Rey was tall and thin, and he did look as if he needed a feeding. There had been some talk about a new woman out at the ranch recently who was rather mysterious. But if they had a cook with arthritis, she surely wasn't a young cook.

Nancy went to fill the prescriptions.

''Sorry,'' Rey muttered as he glanced behind him and Leo at the people they'd rushed past to get their prescription filled. He tried to smile. He wasn't really good at it. He cleared his throat self-consciously. ''Chocolates,'' he reminded Leo.

''Right over there,'' Leo agreed somberly. ''We'd better get two boxes. And some of that cream stuff for arthritis, and there's some sort of joint formula...''

''And the We're Sorry card,'' Rey added, mumbling something about shortsightedness and loose tongues as they stomped off down the aisle with two pairs of spurs jingling musically from the heels of their boots.

Nancy handed Micah the credit card receipt, which he signed and gave Callie a pert grin as she went back to work.

Callie followed Micah out the door, letting loose

a barrage of laughter when they reached the Porsche. By the time they got to her apartment, he was laughing, too, at the town's most notorious biscuit eaters.

Jack Steele was overjoyed at the news they had for him. For the next week he perked up as never before, taking a new interest in life and looking forward to having a daughter-in-law and a grandchild. The news that he was going to live with them disturbed him, he thought they needed privacy, but they insisted. He gave in. There was no mistaking their genuine love for him, or their delight in his company. He felt like the richest man on earth.

Callie, meanwhile, had an unexpected phone call from her father, who was back in town and anxious to see her. She met him in Barbara's café on her lunch hour from the law office, curious and nervous after so many years away from him.

Her father had black hair with silver at his temples and dark blue eyes. He was somber, quiet, unassuming and guilt was written all over him.

After they'd both ordered salads and drinks, her father gave her a long, hesitant scrutiny.

"You look so much like my mother," he said unexpectedly. "She had the same shaped eyes you do, and the same color."

Callie looked down at her salad. "Do I?"

He laid down his fork and leaned forward on his elbows. "I've been an idiot. How do I apologize for years of neglect, for letting you be put through hell in foster homes?" he asked quietly. "When I knew what had happened to you, I was too ashamed even to phone. Your mother had only just told me the truth and after the private detective I hired gave me the file on you, I couldn't take it. I went to Europe and stayed for a month. I don't even remember what I did there." He grimaced at Callie's expression. "I'm so ashamed. Even if you hadn't been my biological child, you'd lived in my house, I'd loved you, protected you." He lowered his shamed eyes to his plate. "Pride. It was nothing but pride. I couldn't bear thinking that you were another man's child. You paid for my cruelty, all those years." He drew in a long breath and looked up at her sadly. "You're my daughter. But I don't deserve you." He made an awkward motion. "So if you don't want to have anything to do with me, that's all right. I'll understand. I've been a dead bust as a father."

She could see the torment in his eyes. Her mother had done something unspeakably cruel to both of them with her lies. The bond they'd formed had been broken, tragically. She remembered the loneliness of her childhood, the misery of belonging nowhere. But now she had Micah and a child on the way, and Jack Steele as well. She'd landed on her feet, grown strong, learned to cope with life. She'd even fought off drug dealing thugs, all by herself, that night in Nassau when her child had been conceived. She felt so mature now, so capable. She smiled slowly. She'd lectured Micah about forgiveness. Here was her best chance to prove that she believed her own words.

"You're going to be a grandfather," she said simply. "Micah and I are getting married Sunday afternoon at two o'clock in the Methodist church. You and Jack Steele could both give me away if you like." She grinned. "It will raise eyebrows everywhere!"

He seemed shocked. His blue eyes misted and he

bit his lip. "A grandfather." He laughed self-consciously and looked away long enough to brush away something that looked suspiciously wet. "I like that." He glanced back at her. "Yes. I'd like to give you away. I'd like to get you back even more, Callie. I'm...sorry."

When he choked up like that, she was beyond touched. She got up from her seat and went around to hug him to her. The café was crowded and she didn't care. She held him close and laid her cheek on his hair, feeling his shoulders shake. It was, in so many ways, one of the most poignant experiences of her young life.

"It's okay, Papa," she whispered, having called him that when she was barely school age. "It's okay now."

He held her tighter and he didn't give a damn that he was crying and half of Jacobsville could see him. He had his daughter back, against all the odds.

Callie felt like that, too. She met Barbara's eyes over the counter and smiled through her tears. Barbara nodded, and smiled, and reached for a napkin. It was so much like a new start. Everything was fresh and sweet and life was blessed. She was never again going to take anything for granted as long as she lived!

The wedding was an event. Callie had an imported gown from Paris, despite the rush to get it in time. Micah wore a morning coat. All the local mercenaries and the gang from the island, including Bojo, Peter, Rodrigo and Mac were there, along with Pogo and Maddie. And, really, Callie thought, Maddie did resemble her, but the older woman was much more athletic and oddly pretty. She smiled broadly at Callie as she stood beside a man Callie didn't recognize, with jet-black hair and eyes and what was obviously a prosthetic arm. There were a lot of men she didn't know. Probably Micah had contacts everywhere, and when word of the marriage had gotten out, they all came running to see if the rumors were true. Some of them looked astonished, but most were grinning widely.

The ceremony was brief, but beautiful. Micah pulled up the veil Callie wore, and kissed her for the first time as his wife.

''When we're finished, you have to read the inscription in your wedding band,'' he whispered against her soft mouth.

''Don't make me wait,'' she teased. ''What does it say?''

He clasped her hand to his chest, ignoring the glowing faces of the audience. ''It says 'forever,' Callie. And it means forever. I'll love you until I close my eyes for the last time. And even afterward, I'll love you.''

She cried as he kissed her. It was the most beautiful thing he'd ever said to her. She whispered the words back to him, under her breath, while a soft sound rippled through the church. The couple at the rose-decked altar were so much in love that they fairly glowed with it.

They walked out under a cloud of rose petals and rice and Callie stopped and threw her bouquet as they reached the limousine that would take them to the airport. They were flying to Scotland for their honeymoon, to a little thatched cottage that belonged to Mac and had been loaned to them for the occasion.

A romantic gesture from a practical and very unromantic man, that had touched Callie greatly.

Jack Steele, who was staying at the ranch with Micah's new foreman and his wife, waved them off with tears in his eyes, standing next to Kane Kirby, who was doing the same. The two men had become friends already, both avid poker players and old war movie fanatics.

A flustered blond Janie Brewster had caught the bouquet that Callie threw, and she looked down at it as if she didn't quite know what to do next. Nearby, the whole Hart family was watching, married brothers Corrigan and Simon and Cag, and the bachelor boys, Rey and Leo. It was Leo who was giving Janie an odd look, but she didn't see it. She laughed nervously and quickly handed the bouquet to old Mrs. Smith, Callie's neighbor. Then she ducked into the crowd and vanished, to Callie's amusement.

"The last mercenary," she whispered. "And you didn't get away, after all."

"Not the last," he murmured, glancing toward his old comrades and Peter, their newest member, all of whom were silently easing away toward the parking lot. He smiled down at her. "But the happiest," he added, bending to kiss her. "Wave bye at both our papas and let's go. I can't wait to get you alone, Mrs. Steele!"

She chuckled and blushed prettily. "That makes two of us!"

She waved and climbed into the car with her acres of silk and lace and waited for Micah to pile in beside her. The door closed. The car drove away to the excited cries of good luck that followed it. Inside, two newlyweds were wrapped up close in each others' arms, oblivious to everything else. Micah cradled Callie in his arms and thanked God for second chances. He recalled Callie's soft words: After the pain, the pleasure. He closed his eyes and sighed. The pleasure had just begun.

\*    \*    \*    \*    \*

*Biscuit makers beware!*
*Rey Hart is coming your way.*
*Look for*

*A MAN OF MEANS*

*by Diana Palmer*
*in Silhouette Desire in April 2002.*

Silhouette Books cordially invites you to come
on down to Jacobsville, Texas, for

# DIANA PALMER's
## LONG, TALL TEXAN
### *Weddings*

(On sale November 2001)

The LONG, TALL TEXANS series from international
bestselling author Diana Palmer is cherished around the
world. Now three sensuous, charming love stories from
this blockbuster series—*Coltrain's Proposal, Beloved* and
*"Paper Husband"*—are available in one special volume!

*As free as wild mustangs, Jeb, Simon and Hank vowed
never to submit to the reins of marriage. Until, of course,
a certain trio of provocative beauties tempt these Lone Star
lovers off the range...and into a tender, timeless embrace!*

You won't want to miss
LONG, TALL TEXAN WEDDINGS
by Diana Palmer, featuring two
full-length novels and one short story!

*Available only from Silhouette Books at your favorite retail outlet.*

**Silhouette®**
*Where love comes alive™*

SILHOUETTE®
MAKES YOU
A STAR!

# Feel like a star with Silhouette.

We will fly you and a guest to New York City for an exciting weekend stay at a glamorous 5-star hotel. Experience a refreshing day at one of New York's trendiest spas and have your photo taken by a professional. Plus, receive $1,000 U.S. spending money!

## Flowers...long walks...dinner for two... how does Silhouette Books make romance come alive for you?

Send us a script, with 500 words or less, along with visuals (only drawings, magazine cutouts or photographs or combination thereof). Show us how Silhouette Makes Your Love Come Alive. Be creative and have fun. No purchase necessary. All entries must be clearly marked with your name, address and telephone number. All entries will become property of Silhouette and are not returnable. **Contest closes September 28, 2001.**

Please send your entry to: **Silhouette Makes You a Star!**

| | |
|---|---|
| In U.S.A. | In Canada |
| P.O. Box 9069 | P.O. Box 637 |
| Buffalo, NY, 14269-9069 | Fort Erie, ON, L2A 5X3 |

Look for contest details on the next page, by visiting www.eHarlequin.com or request a copy by sending a self-addressed envelope to the applicable address above. Contest open to Canadian and U.S. residents who are 18 or over. Void where prohibited.

*Silhouette*®
*Where love comes alive*™

Our lucky winner's photo will appear in a Silhouette ad. Join the fun!

SRMYAS1

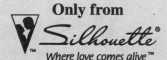